W9-DAQ-763

For Pat
Fondly,
Noël

# *The Labor of Longing*

a novella by

**Noël Valis**

Mint Hill Books
Main Street Rag Publishing Company
Charlotte, North Carolina

Cover art courtesy of iStockPhoto.com
Author photo by Kimmy Leaf

Library of Congress Control Number: 2014955711

ISBN: 978-1-59948-510-2

Produced in the United States of America

Mint Hill Books
Main Street Rag Publishing Company
PO Box 690100
Charlotte, NC 28227
**www.MainStreetRag.com**

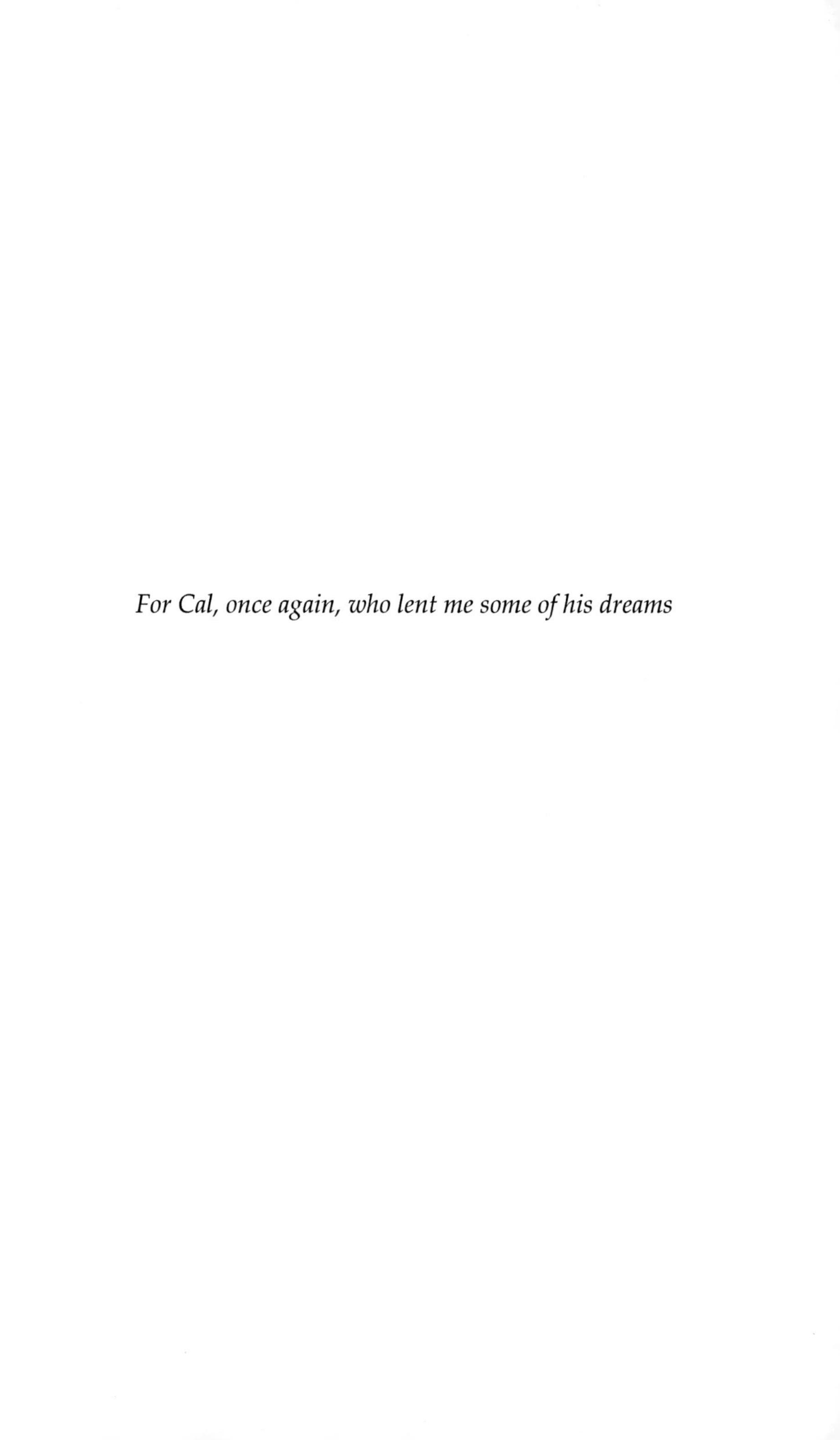

*For Cal, once again, who lent me some of his dreams*

"Of course New Jersey character is in the main the same as all other human character. It must ever be borne in mind that the facts of resemblance between any people, place or time, and any other, however distant, people, place or time, are far closer and more numerous than the facts of difference. Of course, too, in New Jersey humanity there are many places or strata. [...] Character is, indeed, on a low key, but it is fresh, independent and tough as a knot. No doubt the nature of the soil has had to do with advancing certain personal traits and repressing others. Flat, much sand, few forests worthy the name, no natural wheat land, immense lines of sea-sand, vast wilds of dwarf pine and scrub oak, mostly describe it."

Walt Whitman

# *Prologue:*

# *Air Tune*

1.

The fiddler knew his tunes. He played all the songs of the woods, and beyond the woods. One night he boasted that not even the devil could outplay him. The moon was riding high and lit up the sandy roads through the breaks in the pines. The fiddler come to a point in the road and saw a stranger standing there. "Welcome, pilgrim," he said. "Shall we play a tune together?," the stranger replied.

"Well, and why not?," said the fiddler. "You go first, friend."

The stranger, who wore a large black cloak full of folds and secrets, pulled out a fiddle and began to play. And the drowned land sang. The fiddler heard the stunted cries of the pines and the scarlet sighs of the bogs. He heard white cedar weep and wild orchids' desire, and was overcome with mortal weariness.

Obliged to dance, he danced to the stranger's tune. In a circle, he kicked up his feet while the sugary sand jumped and spit. It was a dry night, and would get even drier if his fiddle lost the wager.

When his turn came to play, he was desperate. He felt the woods spinning around him, and the moon about to crash on his head, which was already filled with lightning. Then out of the air he plucked it: a song so sweet and full of longing he'd like to raise his parents, long separated from this life, from the ground. He saw their shadows rise around him, as the music flew from his fiddle. He took the notes from the slow-faring swamps and rust-stained creeks. He stole from the curly-grass ferns and sphagnum moss. And above all, from the confused, happy dead.

And when he stopped, the stranger had departed. With the song.

*Jonah*

## 2.

Jonah Dickerson was a silent man. Had to clear his throat before he spoke. A man of few words, his neighbors said, though he hadn't much use for neighbors. He was all angles, flesh being dear. Everything counted with Jonah. There was nothing left unaccounted about Jonah except maybe his eyes, which focused intently on his task but flew past a body to a point far beyond.

Jonah's eyes were hummingbirds hovering minutely in the air. A hummingbird flaps its wings sixty to two-hundred times a second and spending so much time in flight, can barely walk. Jonah seemed poised in mid-air, utterly still, but that was because no one saw the wings in his eyes. Hummingbirds don't really sing either. They chirp and buzz, and their wings make a whirring sound. This is their wing whistle. No one knew Jonah Dickerson's wing whistle. Not even Jonah.

Watching Jonah walk you saw him lean into the air, hoping air would hold him.

There are three other things to know about Jonah before his story begins. His story and Abby's. His story and Angelina's. There were two women in it, not one, though in the end maybe only one.

The first thing was a dream he used to have. The second was a dog he used to have. The third was a revival meeting when he was conceived. These things, seemingly unrelated, made Jonah a silent man. They were also the things made wanting so hard: being born and dying, and the love-not love in between, which some called desire, some called resurrection. In any case, it's always the dead recalls us to life. But Jonah didn't know that until the time of the fiddler.

3.

When Jonah was very small, his father dug a hole in the ground. Jonah thought he filled it with water for fish like minnows to swim in. His memory of it, however, was that it was always empty—without water and without fish. His other memory told him there probably was never any pool of water and the fish were always ghosts. It didn't seem to matter, though, that more than likely the pool never had fish.

Once in a dream, he saw himself curled up asleep in the pool, which seemed to have the same shape and curves as his body. This was clearly impossible, as he was much too large to fit into the pool. He could only have squeezed into it as a baby. Then he decided that was it: that his father had made the little pool for him, the happy fish, once a pink and orange glint in his father's eye.

Later he learned his father made the hole as a cache to hide provisions, placing a cairn to mark the spot. Someone removed the rocks, dead leaves fell, and he forgot where he'd buried his goods. He spent entire days digging up the ground, looking for an empty pool of water.

This was the first thing.

4.

When Jonah was nine, his father brought home a red setter. "Dog's yours," he said. "Name's Red." He never explained where the dog came from, and Jonah didn't ask. In the barrens things appeared mysteriously, and asking questions seemed downright impolite.

But Jonah didn't need any explanations. The dog was his. After a few weeks, it seemed like Red had always been his. Mornings, the dog waited quietly till he woke. When Jonah opened his eyes, the first thing he saw was Red. The entire day lay before him. Whatever Jonah was, every sense of himself, was full of the unconscious grace of boyhood, that once lost is forever ill at ease. With the shriek of the blue jay, he threw on his clothes and, together, they tore off into the woods of summer. Where labor was unknown, and desire, a dream that had not happened.

They spent endless hours watching tadpoles in a stream of shadows. Running frantically after rabbits. Spotting a white-tail deer, head lowered to drink at a cripple thick with white cedar. When the heat became stifling, they jumped into the creek and dried off afterwards, dozing under the Jersey sun. Everywhere the woods moved invisibly, while they slept. Buried beneath the underbrush, shiny black sexton beetles were feeding on the carcass of a dead snake. Leafhoppers sucked out the juices of ladies' tresses and bog-asphodel. Red skimmers swooped and caught the smallest of tadpoles. Everywhere life was busy making death. This was its business. And while Jonah and Red slept, the sun dipped lower, the dog-day cicadas shrilled even louder, and a forest of shadows threw a net of stillness over their sleeping forms, which melted into the dark that was coming. So time passed without their knowing, and they were happy in the same not knowing.

One morning, months after the memory of summer was long gone, Jonah woke up and Red was not there. "Where's Red?" he asked.

"Traded it for a shotgun," his father replied, with a small grunt.

And nothing more was said. In the barrens things also disappeared.

This was the second thing.

5.

Jonah's father never mistook an opportunity to remind him he had been conceived at a revival meeting, where more souls were made than saved, he wryly observed.

His mother Sarah was a plain woman, unmarried at thirty-three. Like the other women, she worked alongside the men, pulling moss, scooping cranberries and picking wild blueberries. And when the traveling preacher come to the woods, she put on her best grass hat and went to get religion. Sarah was Methodist, but if preacher was Baptist, she'd go anyway.

Revivals were welcome in the barrens and were often conducted at night by torchlight, deep in the woods, which rustled with people arriving in groups of two or three or more. On faint, narrow pathways that next year would be overgrown with yellow orchid and prickly pear. What marked you as belonging to the pinelands was not heredity but geography. Foreign men came from anywhere else. The people of the pines were as tenacious as the scrubby trees clinging to the sandy soil. They lived at the edges of the universe, and their lives ran underground like the rich reserves of water beneath their feet. Foreign men did not know them, nor indeed did they know themselves sometimes. They were their own wilderness.

The revival was a brush fire that seared their solitary selves together, as Jonah's father and Sarah knelt and embraced to praise the Lord.

It was, however, Sarah's misfortune to have been saved on burned ground.

This was the third thing.

6.

By the time of the fiddler, however, Jonah was alone. He'd been married once, in 1887. Fetched her from Philadelphia, though Abby's family lived in Toms River and before that, near Shamong, down by Hog Wallow. She served in one of the big houses, but seemed happy to return. A year later he found her hanging from a beam. Jonah's eyes fluttered, as he cut her down. When his chin grazed her light brown hair, he knew his loss and clutched her body like a man drowning grasps water.

What was the connection between love and this? Was a wedding death in disguise? The sun was setting and pierced his eyes blinding him for an unbearable instant. He looked down at her small body, lying still on the floorboards. "Little mouse," he murmured.

He did not know what to do. As the last of the day passed over her, he saw the body seem to rise again lifted by the incoming waves of night. This was how you made a year vanish.

7.

After that, Jonah took to wandering. He wandered like the people in his dream. They rambled up and down a conical hill, and had one leg shorter than the other. And when they died, they pulled tiny shades over their faces. But they continued to walk up and down the hill, not speaking to anybody.

At first Jonah wandered through the woods. It was early autumn when he buried Abby. The cranberry bogs were aflame, and men were scooping up berries till their arms felt near pulled off. Legions of scarlet floated down stream, in shallow bogs that once had held iron. As the light of day was dying, Jonah waded in, hoping he said later for the sea of red to rise in a thick wall of blood and swallow him up whole like the armies of Egypt. As this was not likely to happen, he stepped out and lay on the ground, which was cold and damp. He lay there all night, shivering like a fool, and when it was morning, he got up and went away.

8.

Jonah went to Philadelphia. As he knew no one there, he found a boarding-house and rented a room. From his second-story window he could see over the crowds of people, like they were dwarf pines and his head rising above the tops of the trees. He looked for signs of fire in the blackened trunks and fresh green growth at the crown, but was unable to read what he saw there. The barrens were periodically reborn from fire. Fire swept over the stunted pines and white cedars, over the huckleberry bushes in tiny cemeteries, forked into the poor soil and came up like lightning clawing the ground. Fire was ruination, his neighbors said. But he wasn't sure about that.

As Jonah soon tired of watching people, he went looking for work. It did not occur to him he could die of hunger in Philadelphia, or fall victim to murderous gangs of thieves. Jonah's mind had no place for dwelling upon things that had not yet happened. He was not a weighty man like the school teacher.

He met a fellow-boarder. Settimo was an Italian day laborer, who knew little English. Though barely forty, he was a gnarled old tree and spoke through his hands. His skin was darkened and creased like a walnut. His clothes hung limp and look borrowed on his spare body.

Jonah took to working alongside Settimo. They were sewer rats for three months, fixing broken pipe and tunneling deep into caverns of human waste. Afterward, their clothes smelled of damp earth and pestilence. Then they hauled coal, shuttling hard lumps into the bowels of Philadelphia's finest residences. They became rag pickers and scrap iron dealers, but ran into trouble with the local tinkers. Mostly, they became invisible.

*Settimo, Jonah*

9.

Settimo's hands were like a fingerboard. In the Pines, a fingerboard was where roads met. A hand, though, was a sign of a crossing that hadn't yet taken place. Most of Settimo's joints were swollen and tense. His skin was vesuvian, erupting in chronic upheavals of bad health. He was periodically afflicted with bouts of pellagra, the smarting skin disease that flagellated his hands and feet with a painful red rash which burned under the Lombard sun and predisposed him to melancholy. In places his skin had blackened and mummified under the steady progression of the disease.

Sometimes he heard a singing in his ears. Or saw things that weren't there. More often he felt a profound disintegration deep inside himself that he believed would end with his heart being slowly devoured. He pictured his heart like a red rose with the petals turning black and moldy at the edges. He pictured his family, who had remained in Lombardy while Settimo sent money home, eating his heart away, hour by hour, month by month, till there was nothing left.

What does a man who has no land do in the city? Leaning, as though one leg were shorter than the other, he set out for a place where roads must surely meet.

10.

Jonah and Settimo set out for a place where roads must surely meet. They began with a corner. Walnut and 18th

Street. Where they sold cut flowers. They bought the flowers from wholesalers: roses, carnations, chrysanthemums, daffodils, camellias, orange blossoms, lilacs, whatever was in season. Gentlemen purchased carnations or camellias as a boutonniere; ladies took home roses and lilacs and filled their vases and bowls.

As they began to earn money, a sense of impermanence grew around them. Settimo, who was now sometimes Sett, worried there would not be enough flowers to sell in winter. But forced flowers now grew in heated glasshouses on the city outskirts. Then he worried about standing for hours in the cold, when strange thoughts came to him. "I am born too early," he said to Jonah. Except for one other thing, this had been the singular event of his life: having come into the world prematurely, he thought he should soon have to leave it as well. He prayed to his patron saint to keep such ideas away, but as his hands and feet often went numb, sometimes he thought he was already dead.

Jonah worried about nothing. He did not like to think. Especially about himself. He set his mind on the buying and selling of flowers, and counted his earnings carefully, but every night he scrubbed the scent of the flowers off his hands. Jonah wanted nothing left of the day that had ended. He slept straight and still in his bed. But his dreams floated like a coffin ship full of silent cargo.

## 11.

In his dreams Jonah remembered himself. He was in wilderness, walking with Abby, and he could see clearly though the moon was clouded. The wilderness had no name. He saw calico bush and pink dogwood skirt the shimmer of gasping sand, her shawl floating like ash in the air, his brown serge, then her chambray waist with the black farmer's satin trimming sharp against the needles of pitch pine, and all that was entangled burned and stabbed and rasped with wanting.

He saw her pale body gleam for a moment, then disappear.

White fringed orchids fell into his hands, and he was alone and naked. Petals covered his eyes, though he could still see. They drifted downward and clustered like a rope of garland round his neck. He felt his body slowly collapsing into the swamp of sinews and blood that was himself. Mud clung to his fingers, and through the velvet whiteness he saw the moon drowning above him.

He fell into a second sleep, and when he woke he was sixteen again, running wildly through the woods, naked in moonlight. His heart was pounding, the rush of blood was like waves crashing against his bones. He ran until he came to the creek, where he saw a small rowboat. Inside the boat there was a body. When he drew closer, he saw it was his.

The next morning Jonah felt exhausted.

That day at work for the first time he began to observe Settimo more closely, although he did not ask himself why he should do this. And he fixed on the man as was all bones shivering.

## 12.

Because of the cold they bought a kiosk. And a brazier filled with coals, for Sett to warm his hands and feet. Sett was very grateful, as he knew the cold did not seem to affect Jonah in the same way.

"This makes me happy, Jonah."

Jonah nodded. The kiosk and brazier set them back at first, but sales had started to pick up lately, and they were beginning to see more of the ready in their hands. Sett bought himself open-fingered woolen gloves and a red checkered scarf. His worsted coat was threadbare, but stuffing newspaper between himself and the coat helped keep the draft out. He plugged up the holes in his shoes in the same manner. The shoes had gotten soaked, and when he dried them next to a fire, they shrunk, causing him to hobble when he walked.

Jonah wore his clothes with utter indifference. The clothes looked borrowed, scavenged from somebody else's past. It was more like he was lending his body to the life of a dead man. The way sphagnum moss holds water. The way life holds death, absorbing it through the skin until no more can be taken in. The moss retains water for weeks on end, then suddenly dries up. Sponge-like, minute capillary cells perform this fluid task, which gives all the appearance of full life, but only because life is so capacious it cannot forsake anything, even death.

Sphagnum moss was part of the economic cycle of life in the barrens. Jonah would gather the moss in early spring for the horticulturalists and florists' shops in cities and large towns. The moss also had curative properties in dressing wounds. He pulled it by hand, using a rake to separate the moss from the dense underbrush of chain fern, pitcher plant, and bladderwort. He tined blankets of moss from the hummocks of trees. He found it by the edge of streams and ponds, along with sedge, pipewort and rushes, clinging to secret spongs, sometimes submerged in a few inches of water.

Moss was the flesh of the wetlands.

When Jonah looked at Settimo's shriveled shoes stuffed with newspaper, he would remember, though he did not much care to, the memory holes of his mind being packed as tight as sphagnum moss but unable to cure anything.

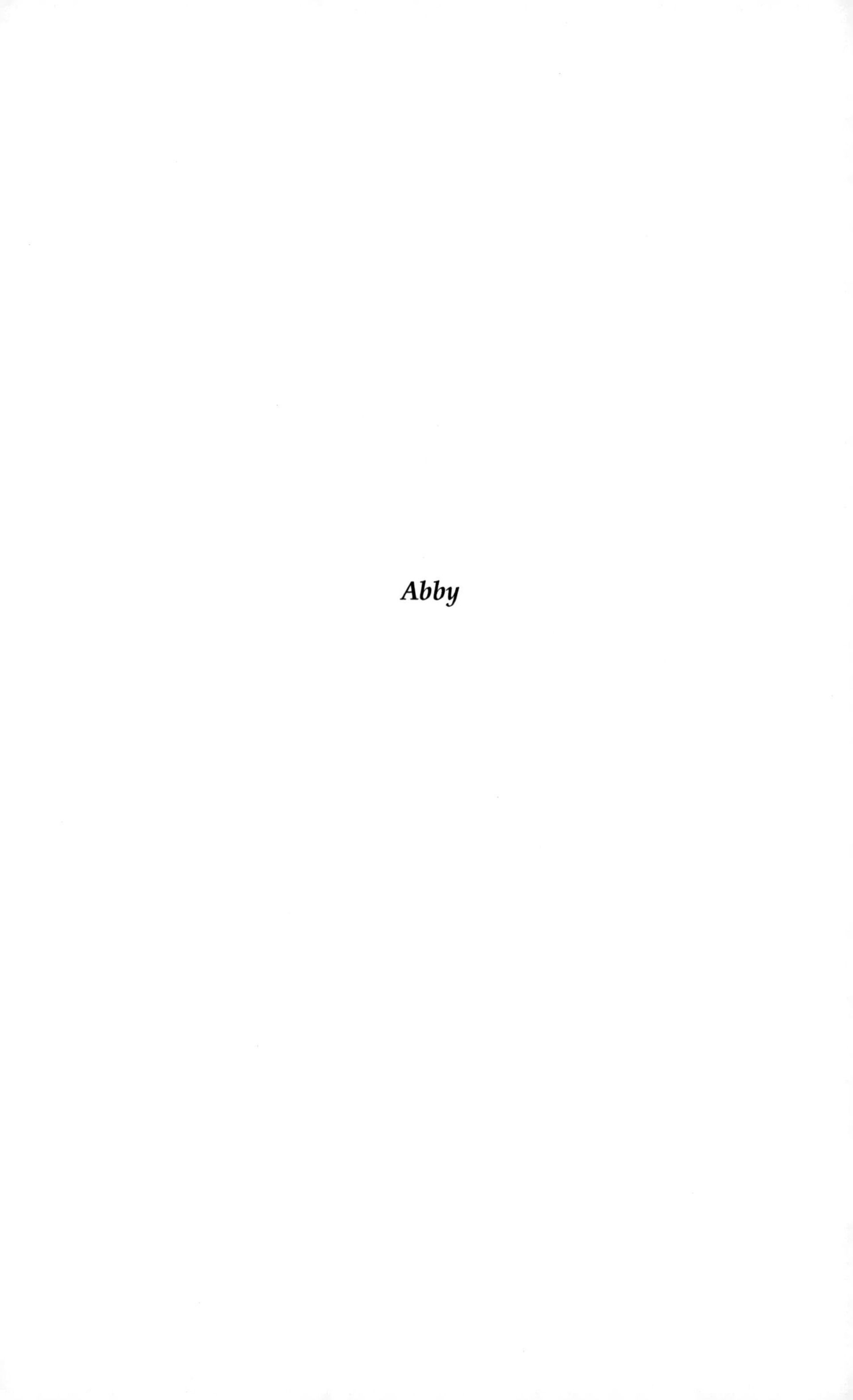

*Abby*

## 13.

There is no cure for what I did, nor telling why. People said it was me that did it, that left and quit on Jonah, but it was my flesh give him up. I see my husband wandering, trapped in his dream and unable to speak to me. I am walking right beside him. Why couldn't I stay? In this life I was never warm enough. He'd pile the quilts high, but the shivering was inside me. Snow was in my heart. Now there is no weight to me. Now you will forget me.

And I wept and wept. Now I am so small, snow biting your cheek, ice on the rim of your hat, rain sliding off your sleeve. I am so small your shoes do not remember me. Now you will forget me.

I am walking right beside him, but I am in a different dream.

## 14.

My life began in the village of Toms River, which lies at the very edge of the woods. Some said it really belonged to the barrens; some said it lay outside. Either way it always figured in the histories on the barrens. Whether the town counted or not as barrens was exactly what distinguished it. You could argue the point endlessly but never decide.

This point was of complete indifference to outsiders. But if you belonged to the woods, you were pineys. If you didn't, it was hard to say what you were.

My town was a backwater. That was one way of seeing it. Most people live in mostly forgotten towns. This, however, was my backwater, and I loved it ferociously and with total abandon. I loved it the way a dog adores its master because it is the only world he knows.

My house was on Main Street, which gave you a worldview that was largely unmerited but fixed forever as the map of the universe at the edge of the woods.

15.

Comings and goings in Toms River were governed by the season, as waves of tourists swelled to the shore. Large wooden hotels and cottages sprang up to accommodate them. From one of the big houses on Rittenhouse Square in Philadelphia came the Norris family, who spent their summers in Toms River. As my father ran a general store, he often made deliveries to their cottage; and as my looks were not exceptional and we were a large family, it was determined that I, Abigail Applegate, should go to Philadelphia to become a maid in the Norris household. I was seventeen, with small hope of marrying.

To be truthful: with little desire to marry. There were nine children. One was stillborn; another died, age two, of scarlet fever. Brother Bill was slow and not much use in the store. Sam was quick and rapacious. My father chose Sam to carry on the family business. The remaining four were girls and soon married off, with the exception of the eldest, Martha, who cared after mama.

Mama was not right in the head after her last child, and took to wandering. I was in charge of finding her. Finding her was easy, as there were not many places she could hide. I walked through Hole in the Wall, which short-cut to Frog Alley. She was sitting by the water's edge.

"I won't come home," she said.

"All right, mama. We'll just sit here for a while."

The little stream shimmered with the shadows of tadpoles. I dropped a stone, making a hole in the water. It was the hole mama wanted to fall into.

16.

Mama's wanderings were more like burials. Every time she departed it seemed like it was to leave one more of us forgot in the cold hard ground. She was the poor wayfaring stranger in the song, going home to see her father, going home to see her mother, going home over Jordan. Only Jordan was here. And it was not that bright world to which we go.

She went to the river, or to the creek with no name. Sometimes it was Huddy Park, where she sat in the bandstand, staring mutely at the boats tethered nearby.

"Time to go home now, mama," I'd say to her. And I took her hand.

"Who are you? I don't know you. Don't you touch me, who are you?" She became fierce and loud and yanked away her hand.

"I'm Abby, mama, Abby."

"You're not Abby. I don't know Abby. You, you high ball it out of here."

She began to pick nervously at the gazebo's peeling paint, as dry white slivers lodged beneath her fingernails. Scraping, scraping, till I could scarce bear it.

I looked into her eyes and saw they were drowned land. You couldn't see into the bottom, where everyone she knew huddled shivering like marsh grass flattened in the wind.

Then, suddenly: "Abby." Her hand caressed my cheek, and I kissed her hand. I commenced to think I was not dead, as her soul yet glimmered caught like the evening sun hollowing down between the rushes and the reeds. As much understand her soul as the sun. We sat together, not speaking, keeping company with the night. Which was coming.

17.

On rainy days mama nearly went crazy. The rain seeped into her head, she'd say. She walked round and round the kitchen table and polished the same doorknob endlessly for hours. If you told her that's enough now, mama, she would nod but a minute later be back at it. The doorknob, which was made of dark glass, glowed dimly like the blue veil of mama's eyes.

Mama was forty-three when her last child slipped out wet and strangled. We wrapped it in a piece of flannel. She refused to look at it and turned her head to the wall.

"Let her be," my father said. "She's lonesome for the child."

Then she slept. For days. Sometimes her hands moved, waving soft like swamp grass, but her eyes remained shut. When she woke, a shudder passed through her. Small ripples of light broke the surface of her eyes. She did not look at us, but at something on the wall. Weeks passed. A pines woman said she was betwixt and between but would not cross over Jordan for now.

When we asked her what name she wanted to mark the grave, mama looked up blankly and we knew. We knew then it wasn't grief. It was the dark glass of recollection she was swimming toward. I woke up dreaming of tadpoles.

18.

A week before I went to Philadelphia, mama commenced to agitate herself. She took to sweeping the kitchen floor over and over. By day, she pushed the dirt out the dooryard. When it was dark, she swept it back in. To bring the good luck in with it, she said.

Her sweeping was relentless and had us all on edge. At last, my father rose up from his chair, took the broom and broke it violently in two. Mama wailed. I ran out the door.

"Now you will forget me," she cried, as the door slammed shut.

I ran to Hole in the Wall, to the creek with no name. It was too dark to see the water. Too dark to see how all the sweeping in the world would bring back anything. Too dark to see how my clandestine retreat could keep away the human misery in which we were no more than drowned land.

The morning of my departure, as we drew away from the house, I saw her small, pale face pressed against the window pane, and I was pierced through and through. Though we were too far away by then, I knew the words she was saying. *Now you will forget me.*

19.

Philadelphia was not the world. It was the Norris household: Mr. Norris, who had made a fortune in patent medicines and treated me with kindness, Mrs. Norris, who did not, two daughters, Elizabeth and Anne, who were preparing themselves for marriage and called upon me at all hours, and a son, Raphael, who having finished four years of university that spring had just come home, when I commenced to work in their service.

My father brought me up by train. We scarce spoke two words together. He was a hard man with a hard life behind him, but though he was my father, I could not pretend to know him. A crow flew into the house one morning, and soon after his twin brother Daniel took sick at nine years and died of a fever. Buried near Shamong, though not forgot. Wings of a bird flapping in fear. The feather of breath trapped in flight. My father could not abide birds and shot them whenever he had the chance. He could never shoot enough of them.

It is easier to evade the living than the dead.

The train was full of our ghosts, full of nobodies, like the tune my grandmother taught me:

*I am thinking just now of nobody,*
*And all that nobody's done,*
*For I've a passion for nobody,*
*That nobody else would own.*
*I bear the name of nobody,*
*For from nobody I sprung,*
*And I sing the praise of nobody,*
*As nobody mine has done.*

I was leaving the world behind. The train shuddered, pulled to a stop, and departed, abandoning us on the platform. Swept into a vast savannah of nobodies.

## 20.

After one month's time, I found myself spending more and more of my hours attending to Mrs. Norris, who was thought to be dyspeptic, thus restricting her diet to unbolted wheat bread and tepid water when the symptoms worsened. On those days I ran up and down the stairs, with a large bowl into which she vomited. As her husband's patent medicines were of apparent little benefit, I gave her warm boneset tea several times a day.

She was not grateful for my attentions. Indeed, when I bathed her feet in water and sal-soda, she complained bitterly that I was careless and left water marks on the floor. When she purged, the throwed substance flew out like the kell of a dead calf, curdle-thick and vile-smelling. Her eyes darkened in fear and mis-liking. In those moments I cared not whether I pleased her, for she was a jagged woman neither happy nor kind.

One night I heard her crying for what seemed like unbroken hours on end. Mr. Norris was away, on one of his business trips. But no one came to her door. Her children lay awake tense in their beds. Her servants turned their faces to the wall, eyes scrunched shut. She wailed in utter disconsolation, weeping like the rain in mama's head. Like a bottomless lake of rain filling my head. When I awoke, the rain stopped and curly ferns of mist clung to the air. It coated shoelaces and pasty, damp cheeks with a film of spider webs. Like nervous ghosts we slipped in silence through the house.

And so it came at last, having taken up residence long before, in stealth. And carefully disguised.

21.

It was as you thought, husband, of our wedding. Our wedding that came as death disguised. Everything, I have discovered, though too late, comes as death disguised. You could write the words a thousand times in your copy book, and still not be prepared for my voice that is in you. My voice which is only the air of remembered flame.

The winter Mrs. Norris died was particularly harsh. One morning she did not come down to breakfast. I found her lying in bed, terrified and white as chalk.

"What is it, ma'am? Are you ill?"

"I cannot get warm," she moaned. "Go fetch Dr. Palmerston."

The doctor pronounced it pneumonia. As she had fever, he ordered her bathed with soda-water and given sudorific, as well as cough balsam.

We piled blanket after blanket on the bed, but Mrs. Norris continued to complain of being cold. I attempted to give her broth, but her disinterest was so profound she turned her head away from me. After seven days, her cough became a rasp, as though her breath were being scraped by a knife. Life fled, in terror.

She died, her dyspepsia forgot, her jagged tears unexplained. That night I dreamed I heard her weeping. Weeping over something dead. I saw her standing in the barrens, waiting for me. "Death is sly, but fleeting," she said. "It meets you at a point in the road, to hear the fiddler play his song." A song so sweet and full of longing you'd like to raise your parents, long separated from this life, from the ground. With a gesture as kind as she had not been toward me in life, she beckoned me to follow. "Who are you?," I asked. "As go dreams, I am death's disguise."

22.

I was not accustomed to the dead, and in particular, to the dead in my dreams. That I should wait upon Mrs. Norris in every waking hour was one thing. But why should she attend to me, when she had proved so hard and unforgiving? Of what use to her were my dreams? I could not shake her jagged tears, but then I thought of mama. I wrote to mama every week, though I was afraid to tell her that Mrs. Norris had died. I said, Father says you cried over my last letter. Please don't cry, mama. In June the Norris family will spend the summer again in Toms River, and we can see each other nearly every day then. I long to be with you, mama. Sometimes I feel as though I'd died and will never see you again.

My room is small, but it is my own. I have a small table upon which I am writing this letter. The window looks out upon an interior courtyard and garden, with a fountain surrounded by a circular stone bench. It is nearly always empty except at night when I have seen Mr. Raphael, the Norris's son, sitting there.

I have found you a pretty present, which I paid for with my first wages.

Yours most affectionately,

Abby

I did not tell her this: I blew out the lamp and stood in the dark behind the curtain, which I slightly parted in order to look at him. As he stared up toward my room. The fountain sang all night.

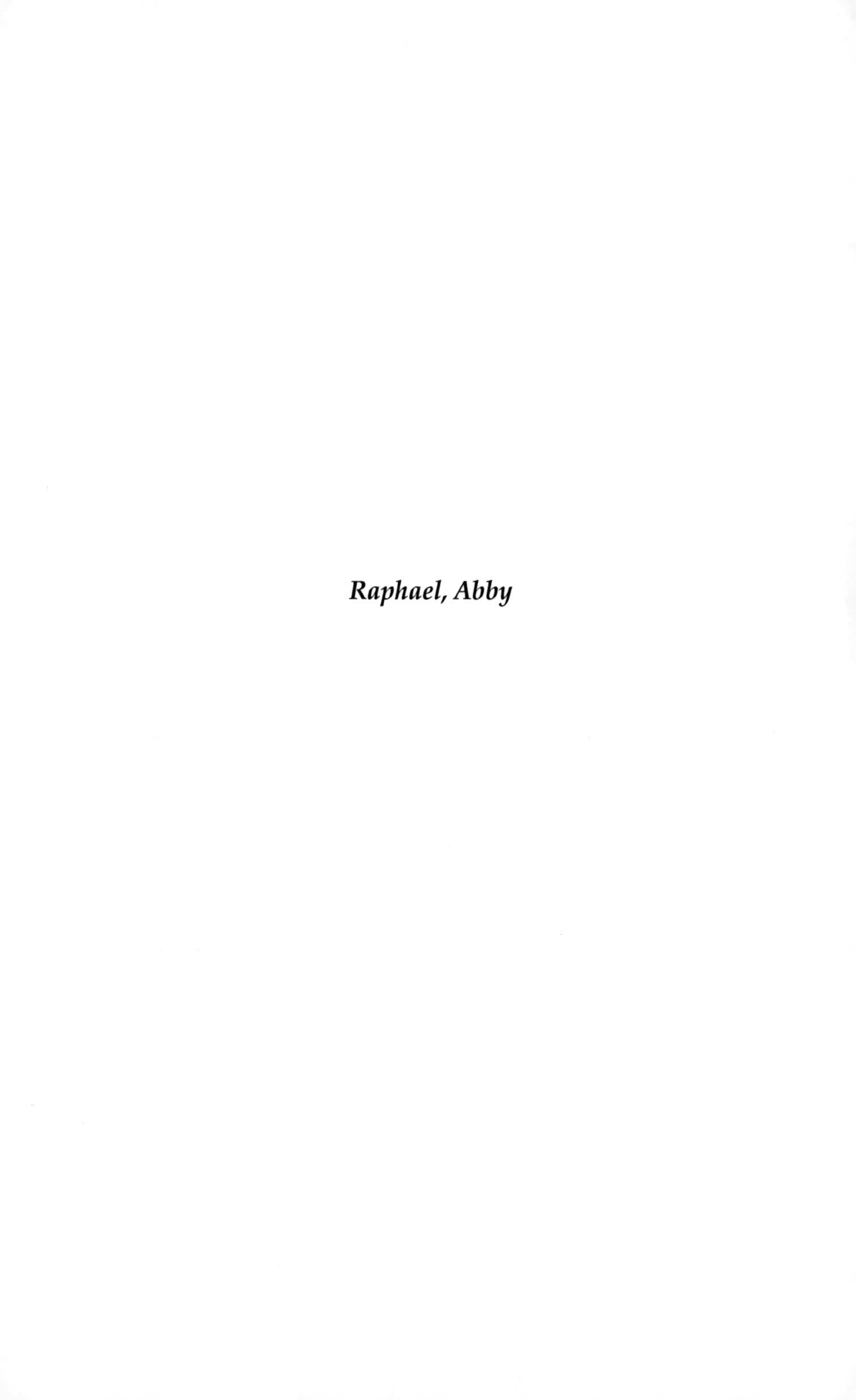

*Raphael, Abby*

## 23.

Raphael noticed me right away. Though it might be better said that in the darkening room he sensed me, as though I were a vessel's shade, seen pulling away from a distant shore in twilight. I was kneeling to light the dining room fireplace. Against the flames my hands appeared translucent and smooth, with a pale yellow cast like finely shaved lemon peel.

I stood up quickly as he moved toward me.

"And who might you be?" he asked.

"Abby, sir," adding impulsively, "I know who you are."

He never quite knew how to speak to servants. Servants who tumbled in and out of the Norris household as quickly as his mother grew tired of them.

"May I get you anything, sir?"

"Um, yes, a cup of tea."

Watched me leave. The stillness of the room waited. Fire crackled and waited. He felt almost nauseated, his stomach twisted, waiting.

The after-burn of fire prickled his nose. Impermanence settled upon him, adding to his nervous irritability. He wandered about the room, not knowing. Not knowing that he was fate for someone else.

From his pocket he drew his lucky piece of polished bone acquired when he was seven and watched his father engage in bone boiling. Mr. Norris's first business was glue making, which he produced by cutting, then lime boiling, the sinews of beeves' feet until they were tender. The liquid that remained cooled into a stiff, collagenous substance like soap and was then cut into cakes. He also skimmed neat's-foot oil from the boiled beeves' feet. And sold bone parts to button- and umbrella-makers. The air filled with the sickly sweet stench of the business of bones. Later he thought to use minute quantities of pulverized bone in his patent medicines.

He called it the zest of life.

## 24.

Raphael jokingly said he was doomed to be a painter, with the name his mother had given him at birth. At any rate, he spent much of his days in a large room flooded in sunlight. Painting winter.

I was instructed to bring him mid-morning tea, lunch, and five o'clock tea.

I looked over at the canvas he was working on.

"Do you like snow?" he asked.

"Yes," I said. I watched the brush strokes turn into blinding white flurries swirling round tiny human figures. He looked out the window, studying the falling snow.

"Snow makes us more sharply aware," he said.

"How is that, sir?"

"Snow is quiet. Pure contemplation. It brings heaven down upon us."

I looked at heaven as he saw it. As I saw him.

No, I thought, snow makes us small. And afraid.

A sudden rumble startled us both. It was snow, which was piled heavy on the roof, sliding off in an avalanche. White puffs floated in the air for an instant.

"I must catch that," he said.

## 25.

On another morning I brought Raphael flowers. To be precise, I was sent to fetch them. He wanted orchids. Masses of cattleyas, pale rose and crimson, with a yellow blotched throat, spilling over in a red cedar basket that was lined with peat and sphagnum moss. Seeing the cattleyas, my mind flooded with a rush of color. Grass-pink, dragon's mouth and whippoorwill shoe sprang up on the edges of trails and streams. I was overtook by terrible longing, and all I could see were the secret spongs of the barrens, thick with wild blueberry and swamp grass.

I saw myself walking up to my thighs in water, when everywhere was dry land.

I saw myself raising my skirts in a scarlet stream of cranberries.

I saw myself offering my breasts like white calico bush opening in spring.

Raphael took the cattleyas and placed them on a simple wooden table in strong sunlight. And proceeded to paint them. He worked till the light faded. And wondered what he had painted. A rich man's dream? A poor girl's longing? "Every calling in life has its labor," he'd read somewhere. What calling was his labor? Why do we labor? What do we long for? What is the labor of longing?

He painted a small silent shadow spilling like water from the cattleyas. Then he went downstairs to dine.

## 26.

It was after that Raphael asked me to sit for him. His mother complained, her eyes narrowing, noting that it was most inappropriate. "I need her near me. You know I am feeling poorly," she added. She did not know she would soon die. Only that she had been sensing a vague but persistent irritation, which made her feel clumsy and incapable. She noticed, with disgust, the first signs of brown mottling on her hands.

At first Raphael had me sit on a plain wooden chair. But I looked uncomfortable and stiff. "No," he said, "this won't do." And he told me to stand, giving me a broom. He picked up a porcelain Ansonia mantel clock, edged in cobalt blue and gilt, with pretty pink flowers, and hurled it to the floor. Whereupon it broke heavily into several pieces. Startled, I jumped.

"I shall call it 'The Shattered Clock,'" he declared, with satisfaction.

I stood with the broom, bending slightly as though to sweep up the shards of debris, face infused with a flustered pale blush, ivory and rose. The rose just beneath the creamy white wax of my skin. Tiny beads of sweat trembled on my upper lip.

He studied me for a long moment, then moved closer and gently pulled out several strands of hair from under my cap. "Your hair should be coming undone," he said.

He chose a very small canvas, six inches by eight.

The convex perspective of the painting, which was a miniature in design, assumed the vitreous curve of an ocular reflection intended, he said, to make me shimmer like a distant dream.

## 27.

When Raphael smashed the clock, something broke in me though I did not know it at the time. I saw the hour hand was badly twisted, and the face of the clock, torn and gouged, was like a jagged woman. Not knowing what to do, I picked up the key, which was still on the mantel.

Raphael was elated, his face shining. Slightly out of breath, he said: "This is exactly what I want." I looked up at him, bewildered. My first thought: I will be blamed for this.

And then Mrs. Norris suddenly appeared in the doorway.

"You careless girl, that will come out of your wages," she cried, pinching my arm.

She was only slightly mollified with her son's explanation and gave me a hard stare before leaving the room.

The broken pieces lay untouched on the floor for weeks, while Raphael painted. One morning, I saw a spider had woven threads around the sunken fragments of the clock. Sunlight glimmered over it like dragonflies darting over the mirror of drowned land. And I was pierced through with longing. The faint violet circles under my eyes ached with small but intense misery.

That night I awoke from a dream and heard the clock chime.

"I am dead," a voice said.

## 28.

By the time Raphael finished the painting, his mother had died and the thing that had broken was splintering inside me like the shards of the clock I tried to sweep up afterward. Some of the fragments were too fine and minute for the broom, so I picked them up by hand. A sliver embedded itself in my skin, which became irritated and swollen. The more I tried to extricate it, the more painful it felt.

Raphael stayed in his room for a week, seeing no one. I was instructed to cover the mirrors and draw the curtains. Masses of lilies of the valley, loosely arranged roses and orchids, filled the house, while the servants whispered behind closed doors. Greedy fingers seized upon dark chocolates of gossip and dipped them in the thick, heavy perfume hanging in the air.

I felt sorry for Mrs. Norris, who was unloved and much resented. Perhaps that is why she chose to visit me while I slept.

"Why are you here?" I asked, feeling her sharp eyes upon me.

"I do not know," she replied, weeping.

Her flowing tears suddenly stopped, and when I looked again, they were shining like a spider web in wet grass. She held out to me a handful of hyssop leaves. A pungent, sweet aroma like anise made me nauseous.

"Take this."

"No, I don't want it," I said, turning my head away. "Leave me alone, I don't want it." As she began to rub the leaves lightly on my wrist, I jumped up and cried: "Don't touch me!"

"It's the fever talking," I heard someone say.

The sliver under my inflamed skin, they said, had caused infection. They said this, and left me alone to sleep, as though there were nothing more to be done. But this was not true.

## 29.

Raphael did not come to see me, nor did he ask after me while I lay abed. As the fever had subsided, by the third night the other servants left me alone. The moon was a sliced lemon of pale yellow. Below my window, the black branch of a tree brushed against stone in the wind. Here were heaven and earth, and here was I, lodged in misery between them. My bedclothes smelled stale and faintly sour and were so tightly wound I thought to suffocate. When I stood up, the room turned to swimming around me, like a thousand frantic shadows of tadpoles darkening my mind, darting in so many directions I could not grasp a pattern. I reached for the doorknob and it wasn't there. The dark swept over me, dissolving the walls and floor, like it was something small kicking inside me so distracting I couldn't quite collect myself nor the place in which I stood. No one can explain how it feels when the only thing belongs to you is the dark. Maybe it was mama's frightened face pressed against the window pane, getting smaller and smaller the day I left home. Or the quiet of drowned land. But no one really knows. Not most of the time. Because most of the time the dark has its own ways of hiding.

From far away I heard the rasp of my breath, my ribs heaving with dry sobs. "Why are you weeping?" Mrs. Norris asked. I whirled around. To find the voice.

There was no one there.

"Why are you here?" I said, suspicion clouding my words.

"To keep you safe."

"I don't believe you."

"I haven't asked you to believe me."

"I don't believe you!" I screamed and finally found the doorknob.

When I reached the end of the hallway, I crept down the stairwell until I stood before Raphael's studio. And lifted the cloth draped over the canvas. I turned it slightly to face the lamplights from the street and the thin stream of moon light through the broad windows.

He had painted me not as I am but as if I had been. I was leaning slightly on the broom and staring at the pieces of broken clock. My hair was untidy and I appeared to look clumsy, which greatly dispirited me. The picture seemed to be saying: when something goes wrong, it is because of you. A ray of sun shot down diagonally from a high window, spun the color of marigold in my hair and shimmered in the spider's web clinging to the shattered clock. As though everything had already happened. And there was nothing you could do to change it.

"Of course there is."

"What must I do?"

But the voice in the dark did not speak again.

## 30.

Later, I didn't know where the blood came from. It was warm and sticky in the dark. If I squeezed shut my eyes at night, sudden red stars flashed behind my lids. The blood appeared in the same way. As though exploding in a red shower out of the fuzz of inky blackness that floated around me in my room. I felt like a mewling thing, frightened and small. Two fingers touched my lips, which tasted blood.

Something has come from this, some thing that must be pushed deep in a knapsack and buried. Some thing with no name. In the gathering light before dawn, I put my despair to work, frantically pulling the sheets from the bed. But then I did not know what to do with them, and there were no other sheets to spare. I spread them out again. There was a large stain like the dark tea color of cedar water running through bog iron. My nightgown was spattered with scarlet images I could not bear to look at. Pulling the gown from over my head, I held the cloth in my hands a moment and then tore it to smaller and smaller pieces. When it was in complete shreds, I balled it up and placed it against my mouth to silence my cries.

Before the other servants found me, I fell into an exhausted sleep. Mama appeared in my dream, leading me by the hand to the edge of a stream. Smiling, she pointed at it. "What must I do?" I asked. She shook her head. I looked down and saw tadpoles swimming, but when I reached toward them, they slid away like glass melting in the dark.

## 31.

By the time the other servants found me, the blood had darkened and dried. I heard them whispering, like droning bees that would not go away. I could not bear to be touched. The blood, my nakedness, made me visible.

Made me belong to them, which I could see in their eyes. I was nobody, and yet they were forced to care for nobody. Disgust stained my body, and they were forced to care for my disgust. I wanted to die.

A doctor was sent for. When he addressed me, I could not answer. How can I speak if I bear the name of nobody?

Words flickered then died like fireflies trapped in a mason jar.

32.

They said I was under a delusion. I heard them speak my mother's name. But what did they know of mama? What did they know of me?

They left me alone, with thoughts that flashed like blood gleaming in the dark.

There was a man in the barrens could make women believe they were walking up to their thighs in water, when everywhere was dry land. Mama whispered this story to me one night, while my father and brothers were away coaling and handing around the same story as they kept watch over the burning charcoal pit.

This same man, she said, once walked up to a widow woman who lived by herself in the wilderness and asked her for food. When she refused, he smiled and a flock of black and white crows flew into the chimney till black smoke drove her out of the cabin. He asked her again, she said no. "Then you shall dance," he replied, his smile growing wider. She whirled and shook, stamped her feet and billowed her dress, and danced the night long though she cared not to and thought she would purely die of tire. "Will you give me food?" he asked yet a third time. "Yes, I will," she said and ran into the cabin. But when she came out again bearing salt pork and applejack, he was gone.

Like a fool I asked if the story was true. "If it ain't," mama said, "I'll give it up."

The wind billowed like the widow woman's dress, then emptied the air into silence. I could not tell whether it was dancing or dying.

33.

When the other servants found me, I refused to talk and Raphael was much pained, though whether it was my silence or the blood distressed him was difficult to know. He came into my room but once, expressing his regret over my situation. Then I heard him directing the servants to keep watch over me.

"As my father is away, I will write to her parents in New Jersey to have her brought home," he said to no one in particular. He did not look at me but fixed his gaze on the wall above my bed. I shut my eyes. The spilt smell of blood hung in the air like a rust-streaked sheet between us. There were no more words spoke, and when I opened my eyes again he was gone.

The ghost of something small flew out of the room and into the wilderness.

A voice that sounded like Mrs. Norris whispered: I am dead. And sang what I already knew: "For I've a passion for nobody, that nobody else would own." But I would not talk to her and sent her away.

Two weeks later I left.

It was not, however, my father but Jonah who fetched me from Philadelphia.

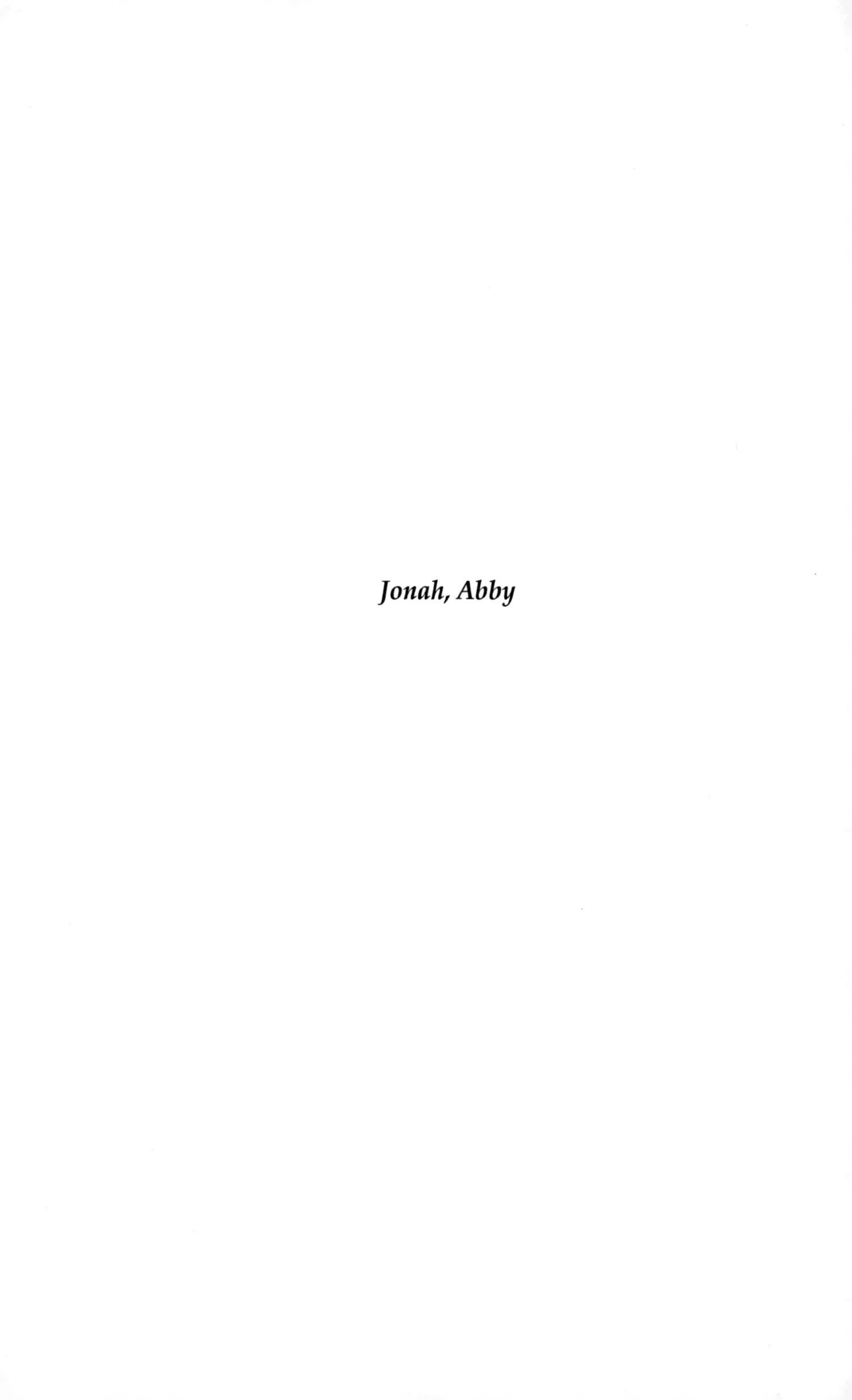

*Jonah, Abby*

## 34.

Jonah remembered schoolmaster used to say that character was destiny. That fate was held like a pen in your own hands. And you could write your own destiny like marks on a piece of paper. The words appeared in chalk on the blackboard and stayed there, the white plumes hanging over the class all term. Jonah practiced his Spencerian penmanship with these words, but he transposed them, writing instead: destiny is character. Was there a difference? He could not tell, as he was not sure of the meanings of either word.

He wrote the word "destiny" over and over into his copy book, seeking the forms from which the letters sprung. All of this was explained in the *Spencerian Key to Practical Penmanship.* Should the pupil "seek the origin of those forms and combinations which he is called upon to analyze and reproduce in his practice, he will be led immediately to the study of Nature." "There," wrote Mr. Spencer, "the elements of all the letters, in ways without number, enter into the composition of countless objects fitted to delight the eyes of the beholder." Words were pebbles and shells, leaf and bud. What shape was destiny? Was it a piercing ray of late afternoon sun? A feather of breath trapped in flight? The shape of destiny in Jonah's hands continued to change, the d growing large, then small, and the y trailing off indecisively, then cut to the quick, in the innumerable permutations his writing assumed. He had long ceased writing destiny in his copy book by the time he met up with it.

35.

The first time Jonah saw destiny it was Abby, and her hair was coming undone. He stepped into the cool penumbra of her father's general store. Yellow pine boards scuffed with human traffic. Pickle and potato barrels. Penny candy in glass cases in front of him. Licorice whips, peppermint drops, lemon kisses, sugared dots, moss squares, pinwheels, horehound, cranberry dips, jelly beans, jawbreakers, sponge candy. Feed room to the left. Kerosene oil, molasses and gun supplies in another corner. Giant ball of string dangling from the ceiling. A set of S.R. & Co. platform counter scales, stacks of tinned peaches and pears. Abby.

He was thunderstruck.

A sudden ray of late afternoon poured into one window, lighting her hair like sparkle. Jonah passed through the stream of sun as though pierced by a sharp blow to his chest. Like an outgoing wave of the sea, the world receded, leaving a human pulse behind. He was abandoned on a distant shore, the sea roared around him, and yet he could not hear, deprived as he was of his senses. It was not life but its utter fullness when life moves for an instant and drowns us in eternity.

Abby looked up. Flicked away impatiently a loose wisp of hair from her forehead.

"May I help you, sir?"

He could not remember what he came in for. Windthrown, toppled like white cedar.

"Sir?"

"Yes," he said. "Yes, yes."

36.

Jonah felt the meshes of love environing him. It was a phrase he read once in a book and took to repeating to himself, till the words were nothing more than a murmuring well of sounds. When the meshes of love at last commenced to environ him, he took to wandering, for the meshes of love made him restless and desirous of running away.

At first he thought it was a fever coming on and remedied himself with a physic of whisky, vinegar and soft water. Gulped down warm catnip tea mixed with a spoon of emetic powder purchased of the doctor and consisting of ipecac, lobelia and bloodroot pulverized and rubbed together. Then he ran to the creek, where he thrust his head over and over into the cold current. In plunging and purging he set himself to dislodge the threads of love that had wound tight round the roiled walls of his stomach, bundled his nerves into hot fists, and turned the pores of his skin into filaments of flame.

He went to a point in the road. Stood there till he saw the first pine snake of the new year and killed it on the spot. This, he had heard, was sure to kill your enemies. Though not, he discovered, the meshes of love. He stared at the smashed skin of the snake so hard he lost sight of himself and of his solitary flesh.

The next morning he went back.

## 37.

Jonah kept coming back to the general store, which stood next to Hole in the Wall. This opening led to Frog Alley and the hapless trickle that was called a stream. Sometimes after he had seen Abby, he'd go and watch tadpoles. Or throw stones aimlessly into the water. Playing over in his mind the last bits of broken conversation he'd had with her.

It had rained sopping hard the night before. His shoes got stuck in the mud, and as he yanked one out with a loud gulping sound, he slipped and fell back into the dark stickery muck. "I'm like to die of tire," he thought, feeling at that moment he might very well sit there forever in the meshes of love. "Rightly so," a voice inside him murmured. A voice which spoke to him lost and wandering. Like the people in his dream, who rambled up and down a conical hill, and had one leg shorter than the other.

With Abby, he was not persuasive. He knew he was not. When he brought her a hand of johnny-jump-ups, she thanked him but the violets lay wilting on the counter.

Jonah did not know how to talk to her. Indeed, he'd never had much use for words. Words were holes dug in the ground. Words were things like destiny and character that schoolmaster made you write in copy books.

In his dreams words sang. And Abby danced, her body rising again and again in the waves of night.

She danced.

38.

Jonah's courting was hobbled from the start. I knew at once that he was interested in me, but was not sure what I thought about him. He was the gauntest man I had ever seen. He appeared so silently in the store I did not hear him until he cleared his throat.

"May I help you, sir?"

He stood, nailed to the floorboards.

"Sir?"

"Yes," he said. "Yes, yes."

"Yes" was a sack of flour, several tins of peaches and pears, and a bottle of Vin Vitae tonic, which he suddenly tacked on to the end of the single sentence he had uttered up to that point.

"My name's Jonah," he blurted. "Jonah Dickerson."

"Abigail Applegate."

He mumbled a few words, turned abruptly and left, leaning slightly into the late afternoon.

"Old tree," I thought.

"Little mouse," he said to himself.

39.

I gave Jonah's johnny-jump-ups to mama. She paid no attention to them. That night, I saw she had torn off most of the petals. I threw away what was left.

It was like that with Jonah. He gave me things I did not want. One day he came in with a whip-poor-will in a cage he'd made of cedar slabs. It must have been hard to catch. Whip-poor-wills rest on dead leaves by day and can't hardly be seen. "Goatsucker!" mama cried when she saw it. I opened the cage and at dusk let the bird go less he bewitch me.

The whip-poor-will swooped and rose, rose and swooped, in the dim light, catching insects on the wing.

Later I heard it singing all night long. The moon was standing high above me, and in the hard yellow light I thought I saw Jonah leaning against a tree. I pulled the pillow down over my head.

And I went to Philadelphia.

40.

I wrote mama every week while I was in Philadelphia. I knew she would not write me in return, though my father occasionally took pen to paper. I did not tell either of them that Jonah Dickerson also sent me letters.

Though I did not answer him, I kept the letters, which were dry and tindery like matches. His penmanship, however, was graceful and flowing.

"I've set up a charcoal pit in the woods," he wrote. He had been coaling, he said, for the better part of a month. The pit looked like a large beehive and was made of cordwood and turf, above ground. Jonah built himself a rough dugout

out of cedar and turf. "There are pits burning everywhere," he noted. The wagons came and carted the charcoal off to Philadelphia where the demand was great.

I knew what coaling was like, as my father and brothers had done some when we lived near Shamong. Mama brimmed a knapsack with applejack and salt pork for the men. They came back ten, fifteen days later, bursting with white steam and stories.

Much later, after I'd married Jonah, he'd go away for days at a time, tending the charcoal. I pictured him in his dugout, eyes steady. His heart packed down like underbrush. Staring at something in the darkness he couldn't see. An invisible gathering that waited at the edge of the clearing, for a spark to ignite. Like wildfire.

41.

Jonah once told me he had been conceived at a revival meeting. Oh yes, his father said, preacher was in good spirits that night, shouting:

"Lord, begin the work! Lord, begin the work *now*! Lord, begin the work just *there*!"

A man standing beside a tree fell to the ground and asked for mercy. He confessed to having killed his wife and hid the body in the woods. This deed plagued him so grievously he had not slept in two years. After that, he slept for eight days straight. They hanged him two weeks later. I had also heard this story when I was a child. Stories in the barrens never died but came up like wild crocuses in a different spot every spring. Still, I wondered whether Jonah's father had purely made it up, or whether he remembered it as something that might have been true. Or was true because he knew it to be so.

Jonah's conception and this story became intertwined in his memory. Now I ask you, said his father, had the man been saved? And then he laughed, answering his own question: hang me if he hadn't!

But I knew the story was troubling to Jonah. For what did it mean to have been conceived, like the man's fate, on the same ground?

# *Jonah*

## 42.

Jonah found the advertisement that winter: "Dryer's Specialties. Palms, ferns, decorative plants, new and rare aquatics—nymphaeas, nelumbiums, victorias, etc.—Herbaceous plants—a large collection of all the desirable species—Novelties—all the latest introductions. Shopman wanted. Inquiries 714 Chestnut Street, Philadelphia." He and Settimo would go together, in the hope both would be hired.

A well-appointed ice-box dominated the view. Ferns and palms were artfully arranged to give the impression of a natural habitat. Jonah learned the names later. Davallias, gleichenias, adiantum, nephrolepis, kentias, latanias, arecas: each of these words opened up into new words that were east of Madagascar, maidens in the hills of Cumberland, Chinese fans, and the flowing tails of horses growing one hundred feet in the air. Names that were green geographies, names that were black, shining mountains and islands of nepenthes floating out to sea. Names that were portals. The mind within his mind raced ahead and found that it was found and knew that it was something else, something that had opened wide, reached back to the barrens and found itself again.

## 43.

Settimo was also hired. To work in the greenhouse attached behind the shop. At first he was entrusted with the growing of kentia palms, which came from seeds as large as acorns. He carefully mixed the leaf mould, sand and loam in equal parts, sowed the seeds thickly, and placed the pans over heat. With the first leaf or two, he potted off the seedlings one to a two-inch pot. Mr. Dryer much preferred a slow grown palm as the quicker ones were duller in hue with fewer leaves.

He also liked his greenhouse men to be nearly as silent as the plants that they tended. An apprentice shopman like Jonah, on the other hand, was expected to be reliable, polite and tactful but never effusive, in line with advice from Mr. Dryer's bible, *How to Make Money and How to Keep it*. This book Jonah was soon to acquire.

Neither Sett nor Jonah objected to their employer's instructions. Indeed, it would never have occurred to them to do so. Work possessed the gravity of worship. The hours passed in beautifully shaped increments like a wedding mantle of floral arrangements bud by bud assuming its sole purpose: that within the flow of time there is a rose marked as an occasion.

In the faintly moist, heated atmosphere of the greenhouse, Sett dug deep and planted the ceremonies of time.

44.

While Jonah poured over the book, *How to Make Money and How to Keep it*, in which it was advised "self-denial should be exercised in everything, remembering always that such a course is not only respectable, but in the end will make you more friends, and more happiness from the beginning to the end of life. You are, then, your own always, and never mortgaged to others, which is a mild term for being the slave of another."

He saw the phrase "self-denial," skipped over what followed, and directed his attention upon the notion of never being mortgaged to others. This he not only understood but took very much to heart, for it was *his* heart. To be respectable interested him little. Nor did friends. Or happiness. But to deny oneself for the sake of oneself was to be a hummingbird poised in mid-air. It was also to be untouched and untouchable.

Mr. Davies went on to say that "every calling in life has its labor." And "hence we conclude that labor is respectable, and none need be ashamed to labor who would not be ashamed to be seen spending a dollar." But it was the chapter called the "Fountains of Wealth" that Jonah found especially instructive. "Labor, then," he read, "is the living fountain of wealth, from out of whose depths flow the alimental and luxurious streams of life. As the Maker of all things has moulded one particle of water like another, so too, by nature, is one laborer like another. Each may take different positions in life, first up, then below, changing positions at every moment of time, fulfilling laws which are inexplicable by the deepest philosophy."

Though he thought little about the Maker of all things, Jonah was determined to be the maker of his own life. He did not see particles of water as like another precisely because of their changing positions. Waves of water move in both longitudinal and transverse motions, creating a pattern of flow seemingly at odds with itself. The water, however, like Jonah, did not know this. Nor did Jonah know that what once he had crossed he would cross again.

## 45.

Instead, Jonah went in and out of the ice-box several times a day. The ice-box in Mr. Dryer's establishment was impressive in size, the glass display of cut flowers and arrangements ample.

When the door shut behind him, the world melted away. His breath formed the shape of silence. He was sealed in cold, which gave him an odd sense of relief. As though waking up in an empty pool of water. Or swimming in air.

Looking out, he saw customers and shopmen gesturing in talk and smiles. Darting and weaving in the aquarium of their existence.

In the ice-box the scent of roses mixed sharply with the green, watery odor of stems and leaves. The air trembled slightly toward fermenting decay. Jonah suddenly shivered. And woke. To sleeping dreams buried in the flowers. He shivered again and forgot what came into his head, moving on to the next thing, which is what we do when dreams awake and then depart.

46.

This moving on meant learning every aspect of the florist business, which Jonah was most anxious to do. And this pleased Mr. Dryer, who commenced to instruct him in the art of flower arranging. Never crowd your flowers, he said. Seek first in your mind's eye the shape you want to build. Mr. Dryer's movements were spare and deft, balance and simplicity flowing from his fingertips. Had every flower its own story, each one would have appeared on a separate sheet of writing paper. In which the overall design would only become meaningful once the last flower had been placed in relation to all the rest. Then what was individual took on the cast of a manifold, gathered grace of all its parts.

Customers sometimes wanted a particular shape of flower arrangement, especially for funerals. Mr. Dryer hated all such requests and usually delegated them to his shopmen. Who made all the symbols of departed life: the closed book for the final page lived, the broken column for an early death, the sheaf of wheat for the aged, a pillow for eternal sleep, crosses, anchors and hearts representing faith, hope, and charity.

Jonah learned to make all these visible forms of sentiment. He could not yet imagine those that were invisible. At closing time, he put on his coat and hat and silently made his way home. In the dark, which he did not notice and which could scarcely be distinguished from his somber, angular self. As he followed the same route every night, the passersby and places with which he crossed paths soon became invisible to him. And he to them. The sidewalks were strewn with scattered grace.

47.

In great demand were bouquets. To make a bouquet one followed the shape of a circle. Jonah chose a creamy white camellia for the center, stemming it with a piece of dried willow and wire passed through the calyx of the flower. He then ran moss around and below the camellia and set six tea rose-buds spaced in line with the outer petals of the camellia. Delicate greenery formed a cup around the buds, which were interlaced with pink carnations and tuberoses. A circle of camellias was added, with more tuberoses and moss. He inserted a second layer of tea rose-buds, with violets, sweet alyssum, and a white carnation behind each bud. Tucked in traces of crimson bouvardia. He then worked in a feathery white spray of stevia at the edges, backed with evergreen leaves. Finally, as this was a hand bouquet, he wrapped the handle in white lute-string ribbon, which he finished off with a bow.

Jonah created such dazzling aromatic and visual perfection several times a day. Stemming was the most tedious, if necessary, task. Flower arrangements were built on a series of invisible supports, an undergrowth of wire, twigs and moss. It was a carefully crafted architecture of impermanence. The cultivation of loss, in which every bloom, every leaf, was destined to turn brown, wither and forget itself, Jonah might have thought, if he thought about it at all.

But he did not. His mind worked like his fingers, instinctively moving away from the center. Layered to keep its fragile edifice seemingly intact, the white camellia of oblivion squarely situated at the deepest point. Creamy, luscious oblivion.

*Settimo*

48.

Settimo's heart burned for his family. He spent his unoccupied time scheming of ways he could bring them over. Stared at river boats. Wandered the congested alleys south of Market Street, between the Delaware and Schuylkill Rivers. When he could bear no more of his loneliness, he went to Giovannino's, the baker, to write home, in the late afternoon when the sun was like dipped biscotti crumbling in the remains of the day. This is the letter Giovannino wrote for him:

My Dear Ones,

Hoping this letter finds you well, I send you greetings from your papa and husband. It is now two years and five months since last I saw you. Each day is nothing. Each night I dream of you. All the time I dream.

I have found new work, selling flowers, with my friend Jonah. He is a good man but has no family. When I have enough money, I will send for you. Mr. Moretti, who writes these words for me, has let me a room behind the bakery. It is small but we shall manage.

I am taken with longing for you, dear wife Maria, and for you my sweet children, Angelina and Carlo. *Io sono preso da nostalgia*. You are prisoners of my heart.

From your loving husband and father,

Settimo Fontana

At night he ate the broken pastry Giovannino had no use for and in his longing nearly choked on it.

## 49.

Mr. Dryer did a good business filling vases for Philadelphia's cemeteries, having also a special arrangement with the undertaker down the street, James Barnes and Son, whose supply of customers promised never to run out. Indeed, without weddings and funerals, above all funerals, his living would have been much reduced.

The custom of remembrance, whether weekly or on some other basis, meant that Settimo was kept very busy placing baskets and vases of coleus, geraniums edged with pink ivy leaf, begonias, or phoenix palms, next to the stones and cenotaphs of the dearly departed. Most of whom had quite forgotten the living, despite this freshening of the dead. At Laurel Hill, on the east bank of the Schuylkill River, he stopped to admire the sculpture of Old Mortality re-carving the epitaphs of the dead. Settimo stood so long staring at this monument, which graced the main courtyard of the cemetery, one might have thought he belonged to the composition itself.

After he had tended to the grave sites, removing the old blooms and watering the new ones, he went to one sculpted tomb in particular which was not part of his rounds but which entranced him. A woman was lifting the lid of a coffin as the soul of its occupant fled heavenward. A puff of smoke represented his soul. As the figure of the woman appeared to be turning toward him, Settimo had taken to speaking to her.

Her replies came in his dreams.

## 50.

In his dreams, the white-flowing woman spoke to Settimo. Sometimes he thought she looked like Angelina, his daughter, only grown up. How he imagined her.

She stood at the foot of his bed, her lips and eyes sealed shut. He did not know where her words came from. A gaping, black hole lay beneath her feet, which were bloody and burnt.

"Settimo, Settimo," she called.

He was afraid to answer, and shook beneath his blanket.

"Shall I tell you what you want?"

Settimo trembled.

"Do you want me to open the box?"

He nodded, then mouthed the words "no, no" in terror.

"Yes, you do," she said, turning away and raising her arm high.

The folds of her gown closed slowly over his body, which struggled then froze. In the air, a white puff of smoke. Settimo fell asleep. Beneath his eyelids: a box was dreaming.

51.

Settimo was afraid to fall asleep. Insomnia lay on his chest like a heavy lid squeezing out his heart beats in a muffled thud. He heard his blood pulsing on one side of his neck. Felt his legs jack knife in cramps.

He did not want to dream. Of the white-flowing woman, whose words he did not understand.

When at last she reappeared, she asked him the same question.

"Do you want me to open the box?"

Her breath came as a cold wind. Settimo shivered.

"Take my hand," she said, extending her arm.

But Settimo kept his hands tucked beneath his blanket. A hand was a sign of a crossing that hadn't yet taken place. There were no traces, however, of lines to be read in the woman's hand. His anxiety grew and he wondered if he was dead already.

When next he went to Laurel Hill, he left her a basket with bread, cheese and an apple. The following morning he made arrangements to bring his family to Philadelphia.

52.

The crossing took more than a month. In steerage were five-hundred and eight souls. When Settimo reached America three years before, he bribed the shipping official to turn a blind eye to his pellagra. Consequently, he was unable to purchase pre-paid tickets for his family right away, as he had hoped.

Maria and her two children spent most of the voyage in six-by-two feet berths. There was no space to move about below deck, and the violent lurch of the ship made them all sick. After several days, their bodies stank, sweat mixing with the effluvia of urine, vomit, and solid waste. Food was repellent. Buckets overflowed, creating a thick, sluggish river of sour-curdle and human dejecta.

By the third week, Carlo had diarrhea and fever. Two days later, he died, age five. And was lost forever to the sea. Though he would never find his way home again, his mother sprinkled salt on the waves.

Maria cursed her husband for going to America.

*Fire*

53.

Maria, Angelina and Settimo shared the single room he rented from Mr. Moretti the baker. When the temperature plunged below zero, Sett sometimes spent the night in the greenhouse, where he tended the fires every three or four hours, making sure they were adequate to the needs of the delicate life he was in charge of. He slept on a pallet on the floor of the hot-house, surrounded by a shining green veil of rank tropical growth.

Maria, who despite her curses loved Settimo, worried.

"Do not fall asleep or breathe the air too deeply," she said to him.

He promised to do neither.

Such plants were dangerous, she told him, and sent out poisonous gases.

"Is this true?" he asked Jonah.

Jonah consulted Mr. Dryer, who lent him Henderson's *Practical Floriculture*. "Read Chapter XXVII, 'Are Plants Injurious to Health?'" he said.

"If physicians are asked if plants are injurious to health," Jonah read, "three out of six will reply that they are." But, continued Henderson, "no theory can be more destitute of truth; that plants give out carbonic acid may be, but that it is given out in quantities sufficient to affect our health in the slightest degree is utter nonsense."

Settimo could not convince his wife, however, that he was safe in the greenhouse. She insisted he place a small dish of salt on the floor beside his pallet.

In the greenhouse, he sprayed a fine mist of water over the plants, the smell of damp earth in the air. Despite his promise, he fell asleep. And dreamed. He was climbing a very tall palm tree. From the top he had a view of the sea, which was swimming toward him, the waves churning rhythmically like the half-moons of arms and legs in motion. Then the sea stood up and it was little Carlo running toward him.

"Papa, papa!" he cried through the roar of the waves.

"Carlo, you have come home to me," his father spoke through tears. The words were like fine mist swallowed by the approaching sea. Settimo stretched out his arms and overturned the dish of salt. He woke up to the smell of burning wood and the faint sound of breaking glass.

54.

Lucky for everyone, the fire was quickly brought under control, and the greenhouse suffered only minor damage. A workman had left kindling wood on the flue near the furnace. Sett woke up to the smell of burning wood and the faint sound of breaking glass.

In the air floated his dream of the sea, crystallized like salt. He heard the roar of the flames and thought it was the sea. Swimming toward him.

He looked at his hands, which were trembling. "If I go up in smoke now," he thought, "you will forget me." He did not want to be forgotten. Then, Maria said, he must stop dreaming. Of Carlo. Settimo looked at his wife, who looked back at him, strangely. Her eyes were hooded and blinked like an owl's.

Nothing was safe.

Certainly not Settimo's dreams.

55.

Or what he saw. For Settimo's eyes held visions. Changing pictures that came into focus and quickly disappeared. Sometimes he saw these things as dreams. Sometimes he saw them on the streets of Philadelphia. Once he saw a barrel organ playing by itself. Another time he saw Carlo walking hand in hand with the lady in white. When he turned the corner, a huge wave came crashing down and chased after him in the street.

He did not mention these things to Jonah. And after a little while, he stopped speaking of them to his wife, whose words now made him want to run away. But Angelina, who was eight, loved her father's stories.

"*Figlia,* I will tell you about the village."

"Yes, papa."Angelina cupped her chin between her hands.

"Now, in this village there are eleven houses. And it is surrounded by field after field of wheat. The wheat is taller than you, *mia cara.*"

"Was it taller than you?"

"Yes, it was taller than me, when I was a little boy. It was taller than the sky."

And then he said, more to himself:

"Everything was sky."

He said this in autumn, when he knew perfectly well that almost none of what he told her was true. Had he said it in winter, it might have been true. The reasons for these distinctions would only become clear later.

56.

Now the houses were very tiny. And the people were very tiny," continued Settimo.

"Why, papa?" Angelina asked.

"To keep us safe. That way no one would notice us."

He went on to explain that the villagers' greatest enemies were nearsighted, because they chose only to see very large objects and very large people. Out of vanity they refused to wear eye glasses, and thus there was a very real danger of being stepped upon. The villagers were constantly dodging enormous carriages that swayed perilously and were drawn by snorting, wild-eyed horses.

"We were nothing but a blur, a puff of smoke, to them," he said.

Angelina did not understand what nearsighted meant.

"It is like seeing a distant mountain suddenly turning the corner in front of you," he responded after thinking about it a little while. At that moment Settimo understood his enemies' fear. He remembered climbing the mountain at the foot of which his village slept. When he reached the top, everything was sky. But as he descended, a thick, penetrating mist came rolling in. He could not distinguish between the mist and the mountain. He had seen the mountain walking. Lost. Wandering in circles. Like him.

When he stumbled into a clearing, he fell breathless, his heart pounding, beside a pool of water. Dragonflies shimmered like jeweled eyes over the lacquered surface.

57.

With the clarity of a dream, Settimo remembered climbing down the mountain. He also remembered why. When he reached the top, everything was sky. Until he turned and saw him. Etched sharply against the clouds, as Settimo had never been nearsighted.

Mario was not his greatest enemy. He was simply the man he killed.

They had known each other their entire lives and had hated each other almost as long. Both had courted Maria, which accounted, the villagers said, for the bad blood between them. But Settimo knew this did not sufficiently explain the deep loathing he felt toward Mario, who in all other respects, could not be distinguished as exceptional. It was this hatred alone that set him apart. Which marked him—and Settimo—as an object of intense, mysterious desire. For hatred, like love, has its desires.

"What do you want?" Settimo asked harshly, remembering their last bitter exchange over a missing sheep.

"I know you have it," he replied.

"I tell you, I never took it. It must have wandered off and fallen into a ravine."

"No, I know it's you. When something goes wrong, it is because of you," Mario shouted, his face getting red and blotchy. He picked up a stone, his fingers wrapped whitely around it.

Settimo became afraid and took a step backward.

Mario lunged toward him, pushing him to the ground. They grappled over the stone, which Settimo managed to loosen from Mario's grip. Mario raked his cheek with deep, bloody scratches. Something rose up in Settimo's gorge then that he knew would spill over into the rest of his life. He was choking the life out of death. Mario's face became a moving blur. Then he smashed it. With the stone.

This happened in winter. In clouds of snow.

## 58.

The difficulty with dead bodies is getting rid of them. Blood like poppies decorated the snow almost gaily. But the dead man, Mario, lay there, out of place. Settimo had no time to dwell on the horror. The ground was far too hard to dig, so he grasped the legs and slowly dragged him toward the precipice. The dead man's head nodded from side to side, as it bumped over stones and roots and slid over snow, seeming to say: no, no, no. I told you so. When something goes wrong, it is because of you.

At the edge, Settimo paused, breathing hard. Vertigo in his ears, he was barely able to look over. A small avalanche rumbled in the distance. Inhaling sharply, he felt pierced inside by something that, had he a name for it, might have been called longing. Short puffs of breath fell back upon the scarf around his neck, wetting his chin. His fingers were stiff and throbbing with the cold. He sighed, this was after all very hard work, something caught like gravel in his throat, and then he pushed the body over, into the ravine. It flailed and bounded from boulder to boulder and finally thumped to the bottom, face down.

His dream that night was small and afraid, but at the edges populated with neighbors peering inside. He refused, however, to let them in.

59.

In the dark, Settimo whispered his secret to Maria, while they lay in bed. "I know he is dead, and if he is not dead, it will be even worse for me," he murmured. For all of us, she thought to herself.

"You must go away, and soon," she said, her eyes shining fiercely.

"But where shall I go?" he asked, his heart being slowly devoured.

Maria thought for a while.

"It must be far away. To America," she said finally.

A dog howled at the pale winter moon, and a child wailed inconsolably, while Settimo felt a sharp stinging in his blackened hands and feet. And remembered how fragments of Mario's skull had scattered like wet, fleshy seeds in the snow. His breath ragged, he had picked them up one by one and hid them under a large rock.

That night he dreamed Maria had wrapped his flesh in an old cloth and placed it in a knapsack to take to America.

With the dead of the night, as the village slept, he crept out of his house and into the sea of shadows, knowing that because everything from this day forward begins with a death, he, Settimo Fontana, must go to America.

60.

Settimo brought the blood of winter with him to America. He thought he was leaving it behind, but this was not true. Winter was a persistent stain you couldn't get rid of. Although the dreams where his Lombard neighbors peered inside soon vanished, other dreams took their place.

The woman in white appeared again, floating like clouds of snow, her feet singed and trailing drops of blood. This terrified Settimo, who had labored long to remove her from his repertoire of visions.

At last he screwed up enough courage to ask:

"What do you want?"

"I don't know yet," she replied, a bit sadly.

Even though her eyes were shut, he could see light glinting through the eyelids, which were paper thin and translucent.

Settimo thought about her answer for a while. He felt he was on the verge of understanding something very important, something that floated like the sky around him, but that he still could not grasp. And in a moment, it slipped away from him, the sliver of understanding that opened like the crack of a closed box and suddenly fell shut. He thought that if he understood, perhaps it would be something absolutely lovely. He trembled at the thought of knowing.

Nonetheless, Settimo could not bring himself to ask her name.

## 61.

So in the faintly moist, heated atmosphere of the greenhouse, Settimo contented himself with digging deep to plant the ceremonies of time. But this labor was as nothing when compared with the way he carefully tended his daughter Angelina, her seasons, the air and ground about her.

At the same time he continued to leave small offerings for the white-flowing lady. Sometimes he took Angelina with him to the cemetery, where they stood contemplating the woman in stone lifting the lid of a coffin as the soul of its occupant fled heavenward.

"Who is she, papa?" Angelina asked.

"Non lo so. I do not know," he said.

"Do you remember her from before?"

"Non ricordo," he lied, turning to his daughter. "I do not remember."

Angelina stared gravely at her father. Settimo's stories of the village were told and re-told like prized possessions held within the well of memory, but there were other things he did not speak about, for which he was a closed box. This, she sensed, was one of them. This she could not get near, this tantalizing thing she desired to know.

Settimo's hand gently caressed her cloud of black hair. He trembled with sudden fear.

"Why do you come here then?" she asked.

"To keep us safe."

*Jonah, Angelina*

62.

Jonah was a shook tree. Lashed by the wind and cracked on the inside. But like a shook tree, he seemed unaware of his condition. Watching Jonah walk you saw him lean into the air, hoping the air would hold him.

Love was the damage. Invisible. Shattering. Forked lightning struck at the heart. Burned ground. Abby.

This damage settled so deep inside him, he could not find it, and not finding it, it lay buried like a lost cache of goods. As though he forgot where he hid it.

It was alone, in the barrens.

63.

But in Philadelphia Jonah set himself to make money, lots of it. To make it and to keep it. To make money, in some sense you cannot think about it. Or at least about what it can bring. Your eye must focus past money to a point far beyond. You have to project yourself into the future, like a hummingbird hovering minutely in the air. Money is the poetry of possibility. It is the wing whistle of labor's imagination whirring unceasingly in the variable firmament of fortuna. What Mr. Davies called "a halo of a mysterious sum of money which recedes, increasing as we approach."

Those who squander their fortunes without having earned them, he said, "live with the idea that living is life, not that life is for a living."

Thus every extra dollar Jonah saved was a pocketful of his future. Which, had he thought about it, also resembled the recesses of an empty pool of water. But he did not, and indeed, his future depended on him not thinking about it.

64.

Jonah had never been one to study himself too much. Thus he did not ask himself why he saved money. At first he put some of it into a savings institution but was not satisfied with the return. He then turned to fire insurance stocks, which he knew to be highly speculative but liable to pay largely.

"No one can be safe in the possession of money, for investment, who does not *come up fully to appreciate this idea*," wrote Mr. Davies. Jonah pondered this idea without connecting it to himself. "Toil, labor, saving, and self-denial," he read further, "are often sacrificed through this ignorance; wealth and comfort are swept away, and poverty and distress take their places; and such people wonder why their lot is so hard in the world. But when they will reflect, for a moment, that the *whole world* are after just what they have got; and every device that cunning and ingenuity can devise are brought to bear to obtain it, is it strange that *one* cannot resist the *whole*?"

Jonah did not want to be safe in the world, for he had nothing to lose. Nor was he interested to learn that the same author of *How to Make Money and How to Keep it* had also written *Cosmogony; or, the Mysteries of Creation*: "Being an Analysis of the Natural Facts stated in the Hebraic account of the Creation, supported by the development of existing acts of God towards matter." And an *Answer to Hugh Miller and Geologists*, which was advertised as "An Unanswerable Refutation of Geologic Theories as Adverse to Christian Faith."

Jonah might have had his own answers, had he known what the questions were. Such mysteries of creation seemed unconnected to his own life. It did appear that Mr. Davies had answers to all the mysteries except perhaps the possession of money. Had Jonah stopped to think about it, he might have concluded that holding on to something was the most mysterious thing of all.

65.

Five years later, Jonah bought the flower shop. Mr. Dryer, who was a bachelor, wished to retire and looked no further than his excellent shopman whom he considered, if not a son, certainly his successor. Mr. Dickerson, he often said, possessed all the most-prized qualities of a florist. "A florist of the first water," he declared. Discreet and industrious, he had learned to be attentive observing Mr. Dryer. It was not in Jonah's nature to be attentive, but he saw that it was useful and no more difficult a disguise than respectability.

What Mr. Dryer most admired, however, were Jonah's arrangements. These seemed to spring from a source unconnected to the fabulous and elusive fountains of wealth. In the language of flowers there were two columns: the name of the flower in one and its symbolic meaning in the other. Thus acacia stood for friendship, the yellow chrysanthemum for slighted love, swamp magnolia for perseverance. These meanings also varied, according to the compiler of such sentimental miscellanea. No such design governed the shapes flowing from Jonah's hands. He did not see simplicity in a single rose, or a message in the iris. If anything, the flowers he chose had been cut as though from a series of blank pages. Had the blank page been a dream, it would have flown away and been seen to flash like a hummingbird's ruby throat.

## 66.

As he grew richer, Jonah continued to work in the shop. His investments fattened into more investments, as he took to heart Mr. Davies' dictum that "the most valuable services will always bring the most money; and in this principle lies the hidden recess from which flows the stream of independence or a fortune." Though his wealth was largely invisible, he himself was not, for he was, to the world, a man of substance.

From inside the thick fastness of the ice box Jonah saw what he wanted of the world. And that was very little. He was content to view it from afar, or so he thought.

On this particular day, he glanced out and saw a shape walking toward the counter. The shape smiled and waved at him, flowing back and forth like swamp grass. He closed his eyes and had the distinct sensation of having drowned. When he reopened them, the shape had vanished. It was Angelina.

## 67.

It was around this time that Jonah became interested in Italian. He soon exhausted Settimo's patience, asking him again and again: how do you say "chrysanthemum" in Italian? What is the word for "violets"? Flowers tumbled out of his mouth: rose of sharon, round fleshy marigolds, moist scarlet tulips, irises unfolding in pearly white trumpets, tawny lilies, deep purplish explosions of heliotrope, pink and blue showers of fuchsia, red-lipped hellebore. Which became in his mind: a cloud of black hair, pale hands flowing, a brass buckle etched with dragons around a firm waist, a crisp poplinette blouse of ivory, the rose swell of lips, yellow light on the high angled shadow of bone. Youth trembled behind his eyes. It flashed and was remembered running wildly through the woods, naked in moonlight.

And filled him with unspoken dread. As though a crow flew into a room, wildly crashing into walls.

Into this tantalizing brink of unknown disaster he fled, assisted by the sound of wings. Or was it the wings of sound? In his confusion he could not tell. He went in search of all the names in the universe, to find only one: Angelina.

68.

For some reason Angelina could never remember the names of flowers. Flowers were vague clouds of reminiscences that recalled the day and occurrence in which a morning glory might appear but not the name. Angelina slept with names as thick and plentiful as a field of red poppies, but when she awoke, the names were not there, only a creamy deep hole of oblivion. Thus when her father asked her to give Jonah Italian lessons, Angelina worried that she would not be able to find the portal of memory to all the names he wanted to hear.

But Jonah did not ask her the names of flowers.

"Tell me about your village," he said. "E piccolo?"

"Very small," she laughed.

And she told him about the eleven houses, the fields of wheat, and the mist rolling in from the mountain. He wanted to know who the richest man was in the village, but Angelina said they were all poor. "Ah, ma c'è il conte!" she exclaimed. She had forgotten the Count, who owned all the land surrounding the village but only rarely came to visit his estates.

"Dov'è il conte al presente?" Jonah asked in his as yet halting Italian.

"Morto," she replied. "He is dead." On the day Angelina, her mother and Carlo left the village eight years ago, church bells rang out in memory of the dead aristocrat nobody in the village had ever seen.

Jonah's eyes hovered in the air. As he considered what she had said. Words had always been strange goods buried in places he did not care to visit. The thought came then that words were places themselves that could be visited or not, but that he now saw in his mind as though he had already been there. Or had already been. Jonah commenced to remember the Count he had never known.

69.

Jonah wanted to know more about the Count, but Angelina could provide few details. Nor did Settimo know much more.

Jonah's acquaintance with European nobility was limited to reading *The Count of Monte Cristo*, a book he poured over much as he had when studying the fountains of wealth in *How to Make Money and How to Keep it*. He did not at all marvel over Edmond's disguise, his transformation, which he saw as no more difficult than the face of respectability he had learned to assume in business. The book itself was a form of education, which suggested how the character of a commoner could become an uncommon destiny. How you could write your own destiny like ordinary marks on a piece of paper. Edmond Dantès appealed to the untutored soul of the American that resided in Jonah. That this soul dwelled like a cache of buried goods whose whereabouts were unknown was of no concern to him.

He determined that if he wanted to keep what was his, he too would have to return.

70.

Jonah pursued the elusive beauty of Italian like an underwater dream. Words in Italian seemed to swim toward him as though they were languorous, submerged ferns that had lost their entanglements. Then fled with the swift-running currents. As he labored in slow motion, he felt the weight of language as it bore him downward, the sandy bottom stirring in clouds around his body.

He saw the shape of words before he heard them, the sounds entering his consciousness several seconds later. As words floated past him, his arm shot out and he grabbed them sometimes individually, sometimes in handfuls.

*Bellezza, bellezza,* came the water's hum.

*Corre pericolo, pericolo,* murmured the waves in return.

Jonah pursued the sound of beauty with such single-mindedness that beauty fled like a woman before approaching disaster.

## 71.

Jonah's progress in learning Italian was nothing short of remarkable. Within a year his fluency ran as swift as the current of Cedar Creek, though he still plunged into precipices where language failed him, like a sudden drop in the water's depths.

Before conversing with Angelina, he practiced what he would say in front of a mirror, watching his lips and eyes as though they were someone else's.

"You are the most beautiful, most enchanting creature I have ever known," he said.

"I can think of nothing else but you. I think of you all the time."

"You are my eyes, my lips, my hands, my breath."

*Io sono preso da nostalgia,* he murmured to himself.

I am a prisoner of your heart.

He looked down at his hands and thought of Edmond Dantès, the prisoner digging his way into a fortune. Into the freedom to be someone else.

For what had he labored?

From the mirror an image stared back at him.

*Settimo, Jonah*

## 72.

Settimo had come to believe that whatever is true in life is based on small things. Things as small as dragonflies darting over water. Or one man's desire for someone else's things. Or someone else's life. He did not know, however, whether he thought so much about the smallness of things because they were truly small, or because he could not face the things that loomed like a mountain coming round the bend.

Sometimes he thought about the stone that changed his life. If he had not taken the stone, what would have happened? It was not such a big stone, as stones go. It was only the strength with which he smashed it on Mario's skull that made the stone begin to weigh so heavily upon him.

And yet. And yet this stone was like a gift. A gift he could not acknowledge, so deep and terrible was the thought. So desirable. A thought that came to him at night, in whispers from the woman in white.

"What do you want?" he asked her over and over again.

"I want what you want," which at last seemed like an answer.

"But I don't know what I want," he cried out in anguish.

"Then how can you expect me to answer?" she said.

"Why do you torment me?"

"Torment me?" she echoed.

And he remembered the puff of smoke that was a soul. Smoke that was stone.

In the morning he found a rose beside his bed. A gift from Angelina. The bloom was so fresh it made him tremble.

73.

Settimo consulted daily with his wife Maria on the one subject for which they felt a mutual passion: Angelina. He no longer spoke to her about his visions because he did not think it safe, although he could not say why. Maria would look at him in those moments, and he would remember the taste of blood and snow mixed together. He would dream of Carlo. He saw things in Maria's eyes that he did not wish to see. Staring down at his hands, which now had a continual, slight tremor, Settimo knew himself to be small and insignificant. He had not come into the world properly prepared. And hence was constantly amazed that he was still here. That no one had noticed.

"This would be a good marriage," she said to him one evening. He nodded, knowing her to be right. Jonah's sudden interest in Angelina would bring immediate advantages to them, and their daughter's future would be secure. Indeed, Jonah was speaking of returning to New Jersey and building a large and imposing house with many rooms. He already had a place in mind, on Lake Shamong. And wanted the Fontanas to come with him.

Settimo asked his wife what Angelina thought about all this. But Maria did not know.

Nobody knew what Angelina was thinking.

74.

Little by little Jonah disclosed his plans to Settimo, and as he began to sense their scope and grandeur Settimo grew afraid. And yet hadn't Jonah been wildly successful? Hadn't everything he set out to do come to pass?

"This is very risky, Jonah," he said.

"Like as not," Jonah replied, his eyes focused on something far off.

The two of them pondered that a while.

"Have you a name?"

Yes, he said, he had chosen a name. And Settimo smiled when he told him, despite his worries. But wouldn't it be simpler to return as himself?

"Yes, but I do not care to," Jonah said.

Settimo did not ask him why. Knowing that some things simply do not have answers. Or the answers are not the ones we want. In any case, Jonah wasn't very good at answers. And Settimo did not know what questions to ask.

Maria was aghast when he told her.

That night in his dreams Settimo heard the clatter of an enormous carriage that swayed perilously and was drawn by a pair of snorting, wild-eyed horses.

## 75.

Jonah engaged an architect to build his house by the lake. He never visited the site but waited until it was completed and fully appurtenanced. The architect, who found this apparent lack of interest curious, had never had so much freedom to do as he pleased. "I wish it to be in the Italianate style," Jonah explained. This was his only requirement. Mr. Hichens' drawing showed a large two-story, stone structure. Gracing the low-pitched roof was a square cupola with paired, arched windows; under the roof were wide, heavily decorated eave brackets and a dentilated frieze. The first-floor windows were long, and the whole of it indicated a rectangular plan enclosed by cast-iron railings. Nearby was a carriage house. An assistant to Mr. Hichens was asked to furnish the rooms. Italian tiles, red silk wall coverings, gleaming oak library, Venetian chandeliers, a Sheridan mahogany sideboard, hand-painted Limoges porcelain and etched crystal, Aubusson carpets, whatever the assistant suggested Jonah said yes. With utter indifference.

Finally, after nearly a year, the house was ready, but remained empty, save for a caretaker, for yet another two months. Servants were added. But still no one came to claim it. Electrified, the house glowed at night like a thousand fireflies. And waited. It did not know it was waiting. The woods were full of voices talking about it. Then the voices died away. The servants continued to polish and sweep; they changed the linens on the beds, dusted the refracted light of chandeliers, and prepared meals, which afterwards they ate. They did this every day for three very long, monotonous months. And then one morning a messenger arrived.

## 76.

After Jonah talked to Settimo about the house by the lake, the lady in white stopped speaking. She still appeared in his dreams, but would not reply to his questions. What is it I want? he asked. She shook her head mutely. Even the folds of her gown, which once produced a faint rustling sound like a gray fox in underbrush, were silent.

"What should I do?" he said, in despair.

He awoke worn out and dripping with sweat, as though he had labored for hours in the wheat fields of Lombardy.

Why, he thought, should a house be this big? He could not explain to himself why Jonah's new house made him afraid. He stared at the photograph taken by the architect. The house appeared to be melting into the shadows of late afternoon, and the front door had been left ajar. But you could not see inside, except for the glimpse of something white and small that Settimo was unable to make out. The more he tried to understand what the small, white thing was, the more it resembled his dreams, upon whose portals he stood but had yet to pass through.

*Jonah, Angelina*

77.

The first time Jonah fell in love he wanted to run away. The second time he wanted to return. The nailed-together little house in the barrens in which Jonah and Abby had lived had meanwhile slipped back into wilderness, its decrepitude exacerbated by time. First wild grass took possession of it. Broom moss and bracken fern flourished. The kitchen table grew furry with gray-green mildew. Leaks in the roof turned into cataracts. The unmade bed began to cave inward, the sheets and blankets speckled in black mold. Then trees began sprouting out of the floor, pushing sideways to embrace the walls. The wood rotted, groaned and little by little fell to the ground, collapsing in upon itself. Till at last not even the foundations were visible.

The house did not know it was no longer a house. That it lived in oblivion. Or that it was but part of a larger abandonment, which those more materially inclined would describe as economic ruin when the ironworks and charcoal pits vanished, when the glass factories reverted to sand, and the cedar forests had been depleted. So that a visitor could write in 1859 that the region, which had long been settled, was once again a "perfect wilderness." That, thirty years later, according to Kobbé, it was still "the wildest portion of the State." That its inhabitants were packing up and traveling westward. But the house did not know this. It did not know it was humanly forgotten, though season after season remembered it.

In the year 1900 Jonah returned.

He was not thinking of what he had once left behind. But of what he longed for. Not knowing that what he longed for had no more foundation than the cabin he had left behind in the wilderness.

78.

When Jonah finally spoke to Angelina, he said none of the things he had rehearsed in front of the mirror. The everlasting yes for which he longed stood in front of him, floating in clouds of black hair and pale hands. Yet though the everlasting yes stared back at him and waited, he suddenly felt that it was rushing past him, moving swiftly down river until lost from sight. There was this sense in Jonah that he should grasp that yes as decisively as an oar about to cut into the silken, rust-stained cedar waters of the barrens. Otherwise, he would surely drown.

"I hope you are well, Angelina," he said. (And as the oar sliced into water: You are the most beautiful, most enchanting creature I have ever known.)

"Yes, Jonah, I am. And you?"

"Quite well, thank you." (But the water said: I can think of nothing else but you. I think of you all the time.)

She nodded, then he continued:

"Has your father spoken to you?" (As the oar glided past the murmuring wild grasses: You are my eyes, my lips, my hands, my breath.)

"Yes."

"And have you thought about it?" (As he felt himself sinking, bound in the watery weight of language that said: *Io sono preso da nostalgia*.)

"Yes, I have." She stared back at him.

I am a prisoner of your heart.

## 79.

Had the heart spoke, what would it have said?

The human heart, being a small, submerged thing, does not know how deeply it is inhabited. So it is that when one heart breaks, you find some of the shattered pieces inside another heart.

Jonah had swept aside the broken pottery of his earlier life, as though he were tidying up the left-over stems and leaves of a flower arrangement. If you concentrate hard enough on cleaning up, you remove all traces of your labor. But it is only through labor that we exist. Through the piercing intensity of our longing that says we were once here. Jonah, however, saw labor, when he thought about it (which was seldom), as an instrument of design. He was uninterested in his own labor, only in what it produced. And what it produced should have no memory of the labor that had made it. On the surface of his work table he had wiped clean the green ruin of life.

Thus the broken pieces lodged in his heart were of no interest since they had produced nothing. It was as though the pieces did not belong to him. He simply buried them ever more deeply in the core of oblivion. Where even dreams could not find them.

## 80.

Where even dreams could not find me. Abandoned, like the nailed-together little house in the barrens.

I was not angry that Jonah loved Angelina. Only sorrowful. Though perhaps not for the reasons one might think. His life did not belong to me. It had never belonged to me. When I crossed over, he did not follow me. Nor did I want him to.

I watched him as he stood in front of the mirror, his mouth matching foreign words. Miming this new language of love.

I had not known he was capable of such gestures. What are you thinking, Jonah, as you say these pretty phrases? In a language that is borrowed, that I do not understand? I felt a sudden, burning desire to know Italian.

And just as quickly the flame of Italian died. For it was not love I felt. But its memory.

Out of the air I plucked it. Like the wings of sound. Or the sound of a whip-poor-will's wings swooping and rising, rising and swooping, at dusk. If I had not loved Jonah, why did I feel this sorrow of longing?

On a sandy trail in the barrens, cradled by pines on either side, I recalled two figures receding in the distance as they walked. The farther away they got the more they were forgotten. The more forgot, the more I wanted to be there, alone in the woods. So that I could remember. And wait to be forgotten. Once more.

81.

Jonah was making his way back to where he started, though he did not know it. In asking Angelina, he was waiting once more for my reply, thinking it was hers he longed for.

In the days since I took my leave of time, I saw these words written on a grave:

*Trust not to glit'ring*
*Prospecks, ohe wife,*
*Nor hope for perfect*
*Hapiness below the skye.*

It did not comfort me, nor does so now. No doubt such things are true, but are of no help in deciding between the everlasting yes and the everlasting no. Now, when everything is sky, there is neither happiness nor unhappiness. But neither, I discovered, is there clarity. Yet there was one thing I knew.

The reply Angelina gave to Jonah was already written on my grave.

82.

The night before his wedding, Jonah dreamed of me. I knew because this time he remembered it, and in remembering brought me back into the life I did not want. He found me wandering in the woods, a veil of white over my face. As I was limping from a jagged gash on my left ankle, he set me down on a dead tree limb, removed the gauze from my face and used it to bind my wound.

"Now everything will be all right," he said, and for the first time, I saw the radiant smile of "perfect Hapiness" flash across his face.

My breath, however, cut sharp as a quickening knife and sliced without mercy into his words.

"No, it isn't. When something goes wrong, it is because of me," I said bitterly.

He stared at me and did what he had failed to do in life. He knelt on a bed of dry pine needles, the trees rising like shadows, and told me I was his dearest, I was his life, I was his eyes, his lips, his hands, his very breath. His Abby.

But the ground beneath his feet was charred and black.

Jonah woke up in confusion, hearing in the last few seconds his mother Sarah, long dead, clearly say:

"Look to yourself, Jonah. Look to yourself."

83.

Though Jonah was not a scienced man, he had taken up the habit of reading and remembered, on the morning of his wedding, these words from a book on the perfection of man by charity: "Labor is not burdensome to those who love, but rather sweet; as we see in huntsmen, fishermen, and professional men." The preacher went on to say:

"The labor is loved, because God's love is in it, and serves the soul as its aliment. Thus the soul loves in its labor, and its labor feeds its love."

Jonah had no cause to give the preacher's beliefs a haul-me-down, but neither did he take his words to heart, as he was not certain what role God had ever played in his life. Or in his labor. He had gone to church when he was a boy but could never remember the hymns or Bible verses his mother Sarah recited as she pounded out dough for bread or pulled weeds from her vegetable garden. The rhythms of her spiritual life were as natural to his mother as the rise and swoop of a whip-poor-will at dusk incessantly feeding from the bounty of the air. Only for Sarah God was the air.

Of all the verses she repeated to him, there was one in particular he did, however, remember:

"And I shall be a fugitive and a vagabond in the earth; and it shall come to pass, that every one that findeth me shall slay me."

Of vagabonding he knew much. As for murderous desire, he did not think even dreams could find such thoughts.

84.

On the morning of her wedding, Angelina awoke dreamless in a world of rain. Through the window she saw a puddle of dark water, with bubbles forming a momentary froth on the surface. If they floated, she knew it would be a good day. If they broke first, it would be a calamity.

Stepping into her wedding dress, she appeared suspended in clouds of snow. Slowly she approached the long mirror and papered her breath upon the reflection staring back at her. The fog of her breath became a ghost.

She placed a finger upon the glass and wrote a word in the trace of air.

The word melted away.

But first it encircled her waist, slid down her thighs, and hid. It hid in the black pools of her eyes and hair, and in the white curves of her hands and throat.

When she was sure that no one would find it, Angelina opened the door.

The day had begun.

## 85.

For Settimo the day began with a dream. This in itself was nothing new, since dreams walked beside him every day, engaging his thoughts continually. A dream was like a person with whom one had a secret, conversant relationship of long standing. This conversation was reassuring on one level, disquieting on another. In talking to his dreams Settimo believed that he was making himself and his family safer. The important thing was to keep the dreams from talking to Maria or Angelina. There might have been an element of selfishness in this, for these dreams after all belonged to him alone. On the other hand, the dreams were never simply about himself. Of this he was certain.

The dreams themselves, however, were not interested in making things safe.

On the morning of Angelina's wedding, a dream said to him:

"Do not forget me."

As Settimo absorbed dreams like a bed of sphagnum moss drenched in water, this was not likely to happen. He did not know who this dream was, however.

One thing was certain. It was a dream of entanglements, for when Settimo awoke he was thrashing his arms and legs furiously, which had become caught in the snarled roots of a soaring cedar tree. The tree stood in dark swamp land, and from the tree he heard small cries. In his confusion he mistook the cries for a child, and then a bird. The cries flapped their wings in fear. The woods shivered.

Settimo looked out the window, and the dream disappeared.

86.

As Jonah never understood Abby, he continued in his not understanding by marrying Angelina. There was, in this, a consistency to his character of which he was unaware. Indeed, it can be said that character is a puzzling thing, for if we know everything about our own character and act contrary to it, then what is our character? If, on the other hand, we do not know our own character, then can it truly be said we possess one? It would seem, moreover, that part of Jonah's character consisted in not knowing he did not know the character of his wife.

Jonah took Angelina abroad after the wedding. They saw London and Bath, Paris and the Loire Valley, Rome and Florence. But they did not go to Angelina's village. They bought souvenirs, views for a stereopticon, hand-made Alençon lace, a walking stick with a silver knob. They stood precisely eighteen inches apart on the first-class deck of the ship. They were away fifty-seven days, and when they returned to Philadelphia, Jonah still did not know the word Angelina had written on her mirror.

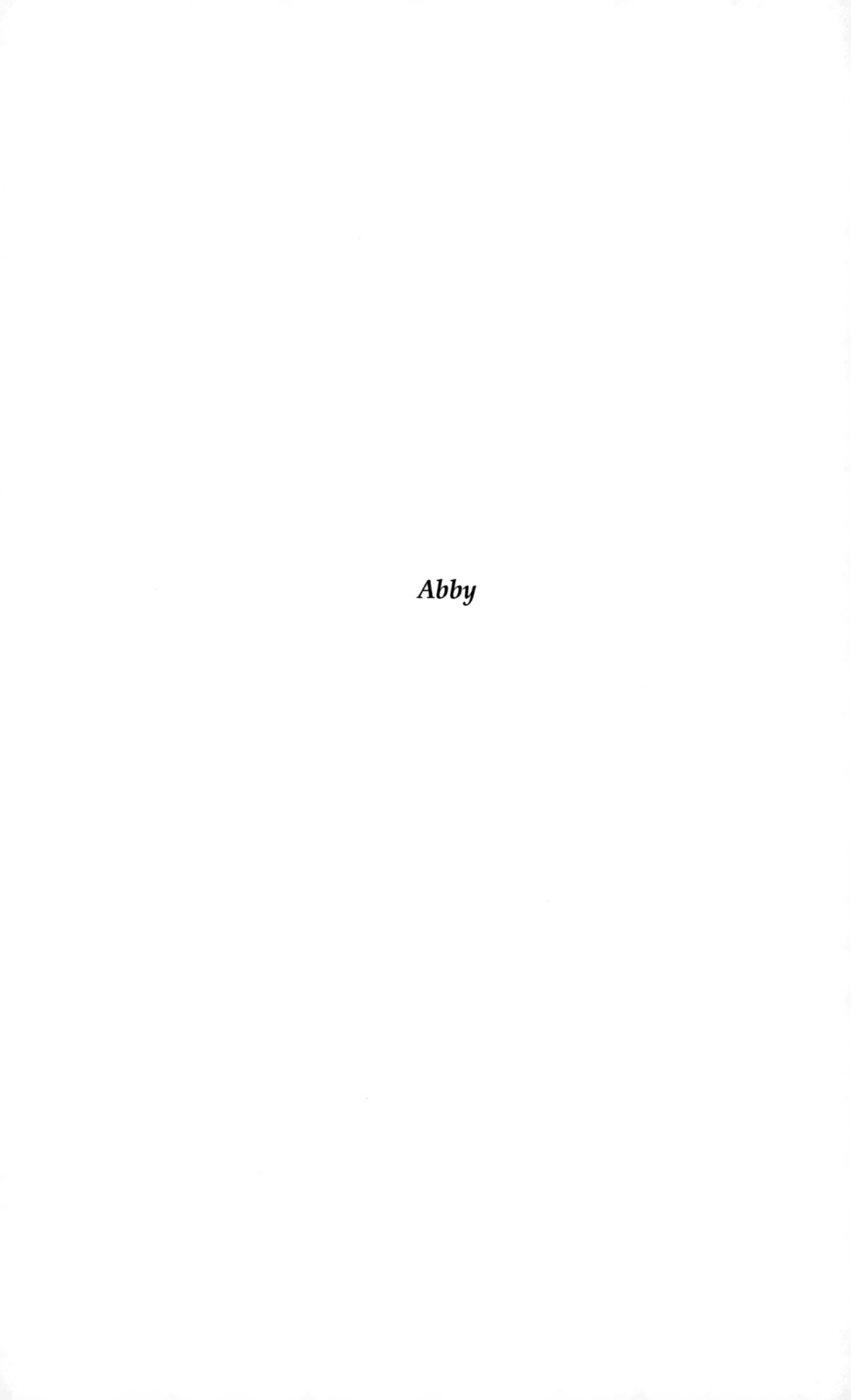

*Abby*

87.

Dreams, mama used to say, are the stories that don't get wrote down. They have the same cycle as work, which goes from "can to can't." Work in the barrens starts at daybreak and ends in dusk, when the waning sun makes it impossible to continue. Dreams are the other way round and follow the vanishing light. Yet if for Mr. Davies labor "is the living fountain of wealth, from out of whose depths flow the alimental and luxurious streams of life," so too are dreams.

I pictured Jonah's dreams like the whip-poor-will he gave me and I released, as it swooped and rose, rose and swooped, in the dim light, catching insects on the wing, singing all through the night.

Dreams are the labor of longing.

88.

Jonah fetched me from Philadelphia because my father was feeling poorly and asked him to. He did not ask my brother Sam, for which I was grateful, as we did not much like one another. We never spoke about it, but whenever possible sat as far away from each other as we could at table or church. This mis-liking clung to us like a wet Jersey summer. How do such things begin and why. As like ask a tree why it should burn when all it wanted to do was stand. It burned anyway.

The train labored upon the ochre rims of tracks, deeper into the woods.

I glanced over at Jonah, who seemed lost in himself. He was never much for words. In the pines, words served two purposes. For telling stories. Or for moving on. Before the stillness of the barrens caught you. When he saw me, he merely smiled and said: Hope well. And I replied: Am well. Though it was not true and was yet another story. How two towns got their names. And it wasn't true either.

But I was not able to tell him the truth. And Jonah did not know how to ask.

89.

Mama was much worse when I came home. She paid no mind to what anyone said and could not bear to be touched, excepting I held out my hand which she took with a shy smile. The town got used to seeing us wandering on Main Street, or slipping through Hole in the Wall to Frog Alley. Sometimes we sat in the bandstand, looking at the river. Sometimes we kept on walking till we were deep in the woods.

My father said she was as good as separated from this life. "Ain't no reason for a ghost to be here," he muttered. I felt him staring right through me. My silence, like mama's, so unnerved him he'd taken to staying in the store till long after dark.

Yet though she seemed not of this world, I knew it not to be true. When the cicadas sang, she listened. She cocked her head slightly, like a hummingbird attending the air. The sound of the cicadas swelled, then faded away, as something in her eyes glimmered and dimmed with the same cadence that died and was reborn all summer long.

One night I saw she was watching the flickering light of fireflies in the dooryard. I ran back to the kitchen, found two empty mason jars in the cupboard and punched holes in them with a knife.

We filled the jars with fireflies, and mama laughed and ran about like an excited child. Then we sat on the back stoop, the glowing jars in our hands.

"Do you see it, mama," I whispered. "Do you see what we have?"

She nodded, mutely.

Something small caught in my throat, as I tried to explain.

The fireflies hurled themselves against the sides of the glass. I could hear the faint tapping of their wings. I placed my fingers in the hollow of mama's throat, which swooped and rose, rose and swooped beneath my touch. I tried to explain, but it was too large for me to grasp.

And by that time I had another question to answer.

## 90.

Jonah chose a Saturday to ask me.

In the pinelands, mama told me, you took care not to work on the one Saturday was unlucky. Else go blind, they said. As no one knew exactly which Saturday it was, it seemed purely sensible to quit work by noon on every Saturday.

Instead, the men went to the taverns and came home stewed.

And as no one could recall anyone going blind on a Saturday, this surely proved to be good advice. Make a rule to break one. As luck was hard to come by, and misfortunes came in buckets, people naturally gravitated toward whatever was promising. Especially if you could drink clear and still see your way to Sunday.

Jonah chose a Saturday to ask me.

Which Saturday it was I did not know. Nor what it would bring.

91.

Any Saturday you marry is someone else's Saturday, as lucky or unlucky.

Every wedding is someone else's wedding; every death, someone else's death. All over the world people were marrying, having children, and dying, not knowing they were the ghost of some other person's life. Though in the barrens news from outside scarcely penetrated, the tall grasses in the swamps knew, the dry sandy roads with no name knew, the bright yellow bog-asphodel that flowers in June knew. All these things knew that in the midst of the vast loneliness encircling the woods there was greater news of an immense peopling of earth and sea, of trees and dunes, that would come and be forgotten, would come and be forgotten. Great news, great news! Only to vanish, like a song drawn from the air. We are alone. We are alone in the gathering company of ghosts.

I raised my skirts for marrying.

92.

On my wedding day mama ran away. My brothers and Jonah went looking for her in the woods nearby having seen no trace of her in town. I wanted to go with them, but they said it wasn't right and did I wish for bad luck. I thought the horse had already bolted. Jonah said nothing, but my brothers commenced swearing and my father groaned in the sheer misery of having a wife with such a palsied mind. It wasn't so much that she was practically useless and was a great deal of trouble but that he could not avoid her. That even if he thought of her as a ghost, she was a ghost wouldn't go away. I don't know what it was, but it come to me that between wanting someone gone and wanting something else was a sorry thing and that maybe being alone was better. But being alone didn't stop you from wanting either.

What mama wanted was to be gone, and when they found her in Cedar Creek, she was drifting under water, one ankle caught tight in a nest of thick roots, her hair come undone, as though she were dreaming. After Sam managed to cut her loose, they lifted her out of the water like a stillborn child rising from the grave that bore its mother's name.

93.

When mama died, the neighbors complained. Not out loud, but in whispers behind closed doors. They complained because of what they heard. Such carryings on, they said, such lamentations. No one could rightly understand why I wept so hard and so long. Death was terrible common and duly noted; and suffering to be expected, but to hear it down the street, to have it pierce their doors and windows, was even harder to bear. Still, they came to the house, attended the burying. Gulls coming inland cried and swooped so close over the long black box one of them brushed the head of preacher who started and jumped slightly.

Sam had my arm in such a tight grip I knew what he was thinking. But I was afraid of the hole mama finally fell into. I saw the dirt falling on the box, and I knew mama wouldn't like it. I closed my eyes and told her not to be afraid, as much as she hated dirt. And then one of mama's dreams come to me. She said she went to sleep one night, walked out back behind her old house and into a field of giant sunflowers. As she was a small child, the sunflowers stood over her, but when she came to the end of the field, she saw a city shining in the distance. She never told me if she reached it.

It was mama's dream, but I held on to it anyway, as though it were mine.

## 94.

After mama's death, people eventually stopped coming by. Except for Jonah of course. It was as if they wanted to forget me. As if I reminded them of something they wanted to hide beneath their best linens and never take out. I don't know what it was, but it was in their eyes and in their faces that shifted away when they saw me. I knew they were afraid of me. What they did not know was how afraid I was of them.

We did not marry that day. When death came as a wedding in disguise. Still, Jonah was impatient and would not wait long. My father wanted me gone. As though mama's death was a good enough reason. I could not rightly understand what he was thinking. He was a hard man with a hard life behind him, but he feared me. That I knew. He feared me because I was mama's ghost.

We are all nobodies and why should we be afraid of each other. Because we are nobodies. They looked at me and saw they were nobodies. It's a sorry thing to say, but I have no reason not to say it, now.

I sing the praise of nobody.

Two months passed. Then Jonah come and took me away.

## 95.

He took me away to marry and, some say, to forget.

Some say as well that after a while you forget what somebody who's died looked like, you forget the sound of their voice. But mama's face came to me in a cloud of dreams. I heard her voice inside me, more clearly than my own, which seemed to fade with each passing day. If I said mama told me this or some thing else, it was surely imagined, as that other thing back in Philadelphia was that nobody spoke about. After some time had passed, however, I began to think more and more that what people called my delusions were only so because *they* didn't see them.

Who I talked to was my business, not theirs.

The woods, mama said, were full of messengers who'd come and gone.

But sometimes one returned, and the ghost of something small flew into the wilderness. Mama told me I should go and find it. She told me in the dark, which I took to be her arms around me, her face pressed against mine, like she would never leave me again.

96.

When the only thing belongs to you is the dark, it is easy to imagine how many different kinds of dark there are. When night came to the barrens, it was a large black cloak full of folds and secrets and rustled like the sound of wings against windows, as it did on the first night I spent with Jonah.

Jonah's house was nailed together on borrowings from half-rotted barns, the burned-out foundations of ironworks, and broken stone from graveyards lost in the pines. It was everything forgot and abandoned. There was no name where he lived. Just a hidey sunk deep in the thick woody mesh of dead leaves, pine needles, and wild grass.

Some of the timber in the house was cedar, which sweetened the air with its damp remembered smell of longing for the swamps in which it grew.

My first night in his house was also full of longing.

By morning I knew I had fallen into one of mama's dark holes.

## 97.

I own the dark now, but what good does the dark do. I own the dark, but when the dark's the only thing belongs to you doesn't explain why it is our fate to choose what we do not want. I do not think even mama really wanted to die.

I was in darkness before and am again. Jonah came home at dusk and saw me sitting alone in the kitchen, saw I hadn't fixed his dinner, hadn't put up my hair or lit the kerosene lamp. He saw all this, said nothing, but lit the lamp, set out yesterday's cornbread and threw some eggs on the fry pan. My father would have yanked me out of the chair, saying you lazy bones, shiftless god-forsaken woman, but Jonah said nothing. I closed my eyes, thinking to die of the tire. Thinking it was painful to draw breath when the spirit is so low. Wanting to give up the ghost, and knowing that the labor of longing had already turned me into one.

It is hard to long for something that will keep you from longing. But it is harder still to keep on longing. Maybe this is what makes us choose what we do not want. Kill me now, Lord, and let me be eaten by the shadows of night. Which was coming.

## 98.

I never spoke to Jonah about Philadelphia. And he never asked, though he had been told, and I do believe he took it for the truth. That I had visioned something small being pushed deep in a knapsack and buried. I had visioned something growing inside me. It was a thing come on me like the meshes of environing love.

Which was why the blood began to flow again in my mind.

Why sand began to drift like pulverized bones into the cabin.

And why Mrs. Norris held out to me a broom in my dreams. It was not a city broom but a thing put together from twigs and switches and tied to a long branch.

"You'll need to tidy up this business of bones," she said.

As it was not well with my soul, I commenced to sweep.

The sand, as it was swept away, flew into the air and floated like white puffs of smoke.

"I must catch that," he said.

99.

That morning began with sweeping the kitchen floor.

When the dark's the only thing belongs to you, you become invisible and only in dreams do you see yourself. I could not rightly understand why people did not see that I was invisible. In Toms River I recollected standing alone in the middle of Main Street before the sun rose and feeling I was already gone, like being swallowed up by fog. But me seeing things they said weren't there was just what made it hard for them *not* to see me. I commenced to think that even being nobody people still see you if that is how they choose to remember you. Even being nobody is somebody. It's the somebody they do not want to remember. I was nobody's memory. Such thoughts would seep out of me like blood on a sheet till it was soaked through. I could not stop the blood from flowing.

That morning began with sweeping the kitchen floor.

It did not begin with dying.

As I recollect the day, it did not seem like a dream then, but now I think on it perhaps it was. For even the dead cannot believe they are dead.

100.

It did not seem like a dream then, but now I think on it perhaps it was. Mama come to me that day, and her field of giant sunflowers. I felt wore out and when I closed my eyes, I saw the field and pictured mama as a little girl. The wind was blowing her fine hair into her eyes, and she was swaying a little as the air held her in its twisty grasp; but at the same time she seemed as still as crisp week-old snow laying frozen on the hummocks and branches of the barrens. Still and quiet she was in my mind, which could not bring her to move on or walk to the edge of the brown and golden yellow field. There was a look of longing on her face, which never left her.

But I knew nothing of mama's childhood.

I knew nothing of my own, the glimpses and flashes of the past adding up to the brief glow of fireflies fleeing from a child's hands and a voice saying, I must catch that.

I only knew that I was alone in the gathering company of ghosts. I asked mama how I should leave.

101.

I could go by water or I could go by air that day. Those who went by water chose the sea as a calling, but water meant something else to me, as it did for mama. Water followed us in everything we did, when we slipped through Hole in the Wall to the sleeveboard creek, when it rained in steady torrents and drove mama crazy, when we took to the woods and looked for tadpoles or wild orchids hidden in spongs and cripples, in meadows of long grasses and marshes next to streams known as drowned land. Water ran beneath the parched, acidic soil of the barrens, it ran through our veins and took over our dreams. It flowed through mama's memory until it couldn't no more and turned into dried-up sluices of lost time. The water ran and ran and finally called her home.

But I did not go by water that day.

Instead I swept the kitchen floor till it was bare and clean. I tidied up the dishes, folded the quilt and placed it at the foot of the bed after having removed one of the sheets, brushed my hair and put it up so there were no loose ends. I tore up a part of the bed sheet what I thought would be sufficient and knotted it to the beam, which I could just reach from the loft. I would go by air.

102.

The sweeping made it come. I swept the dirt out the dooryard but didn't bring it back when it was dark. Instead the thoughts that filled the house took over and I was full of cry. I stood there, the broom in my hands, shaking and weeping. Because the picture come into my head, and there it was, the broken clock, spider threads shining with the rays of the sun, and him painting me, not as I am but as if I had been. Pale violet circles of misery beneath my eyes. A voice saying I must catch that. But I didn't know what it was because the voice was shivering and scared and didn't know either what it was.

The twigs and branches of the broom scraped and whispered against the floor, and I bent low to catch what they were saying. But it was like they didn't want to tell me, like a child playing hide-and-seek you couldn't find. Tell me, tell me, I said, and when at last I heard it, I knew what to do.

A song that sweet and full of pain could only be found in the barrens. It lay there season after season waiting for someone to pluck it from the piercing scent of pine and from the mossy flesh of the earth, from the fresh, unstrained air and from the bogs that waited for the squeak of snow under leather boots to pass. I let go the broom and took off my apron. Stood on the kitchen chair and placed the knotted sheet around my neck. Then waited, listening to the last heart beats of the world.

No one told me it would tear my soul to pieces.

103.

Or that this was only the beginning. It was mama told me I should go and find it. I did not know I would have to die before I did. The woods, she said, were full of messengers who had come and gone. But there was nothing then told me I was one of them.

"Tell me what I should say, mama."

Mama looked at me blankly, her eyes was drowned land. And I saw she had forgotten who I was.

"I am the Life," she started to say, then stopped.

But I am nobody, mama. I am nobody.

Then think just now of nobody, and all that nobody's done, she whispered.

The woods were full of voices that rose and fell as the morning commenced to light. My voice joined theirs in a vast song of burned wilderness and dead towns, and from a trace of air I plucked the word Angelina had written before it melted away.

104.

If the servants had paid attention, they would have known the woods were full of messengers who'd come and gone. Mama claimed her family had Indian blood, and the Lenape were the first messengers in the barrens. When I asked her what messages they carried, she replied she did not rightly know, only that the woods were full of voices that rose and fell as the morning commenced to light.

I was convinced that these were the voices of all the towns had grown down in the pinelands. There were more towns that had vanished in the barrens than roads to come by. Only their names were left, and some cases not even that: Speedwell, Collier's Mill, Ong's Hat, Woodmansie,

Prospertown, Archer's Corner, Catawba, Calico, Hog Wallow. When the mills and furnaces failed, the people packed up and left. The ones stayed were scrabble poor. It was hard making a living in the barrens. But it was harder yet to leave.

On occasion we heard from the ones gone away. They sent letters saying how they'd prospered, what fine conveniences the cities had, how the streets bustled and roared.

But they knew that never again would people leave them alone.

*Jonah, Angelina*

105.

When the messenger arrived at the big house by the lake, the servants suddenly got tremendously excited. Something new, something new! They swept the Aubusson carpets, they polished the heavy silver cutlery and scrubbed the kitchen floor for at least the tenth time. The chandeliers gleamed like shining spider webs, the mirrors sent out shifting, mysterious signals as the flow of servants swept past in a murmuring daze. At last someone was coming, someone was coming. The cook's chin wobbled with joy, and the maids, two cousins from Tuckerton, shook like Jersey geese, their lips trembling. Only two days' notice, how could they ever be ready.

But of course they had been ready for all the Tuesdays, Wednesdays, and Sundays of the month. And the house, which had also been waiting, was ready. The hallway clock boomed and ticked so loud it sounded like an explosion of time going off. Lilacs on the sideboard hung sideways in delirious intoxication. The grand winding staircase shimmered like a mirage ascending heavenward.

On Saturday at two o'clock in the afternoon precisely, the Count Donnafugata, his wife and family stepped out of their carriage, like the next page in a picture book. They needed a good fire to warm them, they said shivering, as the month of June had been unseasonably cool and damp that year.

## 106.

That night Jonah removed the trappings of the Count and, worn out from being who he was, slept. And dreamed. He dreamed of all the things that keep us here, including the dead. He felt a deep shudder pass through his body, and thought (though he did not remember this in waking), if the dead recall us to life, why do we fear the dead?

Is it because when there's nothing more to keep us here, it gets cold. Our mouths fly open, and our eyes look up. Our faces sink downward and collapse. The flesh ferments and disappears like glass melting in the dark.

We flee, like beauty before approaching disaster, not knowing that disaster lies within us and begins its work almost immediately. We flee, but leave something behind. The labor of longing that brings us into the world continues long after we have left it, but it goes on without us.

Jonah had held disaster in his arms, had breathed the scent of its hair and skin, then buried it in a hole. Longing, however, stood by and watched helplessly, knowing all along that it is our fate to put those we love into the belly of the earth and then hope for their escape.

## 107.

But of course the Count Donnafugata was not thinking of disaster. No one knew what he was thinking. The Count possessed an elegantly shaped beard. Jonah did not. He wore a beautifully lined black cape and flourished a walking stick with a silver knob. Jonah did not. The Count wore a monocle, was imperious and barked out orders. Jonah did not. The Count was at home in his domain, while Jonah had no idea at all what home meant.

And yet Jonah knew perfectly well who he was, as it is considerably easier to be someone else than to inhabit ourselves.

His wife and in-laws, however, were confused and as a result played their roles badly.

Strange, but no one recognized Jonah. It was true that he had never lived in this particular town, but one day he saw someone he knew from Toms River stare at him for a long moment. Then the man brushed impatiently at his head as though there were cobwebs and moved on. The townspeople of course saw what they wanted to see, and who was to say otherwise.

In honor of the illustrious personage who had elected to take up residence with them, they renamed the town Chatsworth.

But the Lenni Lenape called it Shamong, or Oschummo, the place of horn, through which dreams like great white stags pass. As there were two towns at one time called Shamong, however, it was not clear to which one the dreams belonged.

## 108.

While Jonah strode confidently through the halls and rooms of his new house, his wife and her parents wandered like refugees in a deserted city. Settimo complained it was too large, Maria that she had nothing to do, and Angelina, well, Angelina said nothing.

At night the house sighed and moaned and made the small comforting sounds of a matron's weary body sinking into bed, but Angelina said nothing.

At night the house dreamed that it was not a house, while Angelina did not dream at all. It dreamed of white calico bush and wild orchids that were called rose pogonia, little ladies' tresses, and dragon's mouth; it dreamed of swift-running, tea-colored streams and tangled roots of cedar submerged in water; it dreamed of drowned land and secret spongs, of fire and air. It dreamed of everything that was not man and, dreaming, found what man desires.

At 5 o'clock in the morning, it dreamed of a house that had fallen away into the wilderness. Of a house that did not know it was no longer a house. It was a dream overrun with weeds and mold, wild grass and floating fern.

And at the deepest point of its dream: a soft, silky-white camellia that did not know or remember why it was here.

109.

It was not clear why Jonah wanted to be somebody else. Perhaps it is more accurate to say that everyone wants to be somebody else, although some would at once declare it to be nonsense. Yet there is a longing in the human heart so secret that no one knows it is there. Or if we do, we give it another name. And find it in places other than the heart.

Jonah was not a weighty man, and hence did not dwell on such things in his waking hours. But words, he discovered, were places in themselves, being empty pools of water that you could fill with anything you liked, including yourself. First of course you had to find the empty pool of water.

The Count Donnafugata had no such illusions. As words were the man, so the Count knew that everything he said existed in order to be someone else. It did not matter that he himself had no idea at all who he was.

From the gleaming silver knob of his walking stick came pictures of a village he had never seen.

110.

Angelina, on the other hand, did not know she was a mystery. Nor did Jonah, though had he thought about it, he would have realized that he coveted his own wife, and in coveting her, made her the mysterious object of unapproachable beauty. He stared at her for hours while she slept. He stared at her when she spoke with Settimo and Maria. When the stable boy Arnaldo held the stirrup to her favorite horse as she mounted. When she leaned over to cut flowers from the garden. His eyes were windows and doorways; his eyes were the dark. What was Angelina thinking? Did she think about him? Did her hands remember his? Did her eyes see his?

He wore himself out looking at her.

A month after their arrival, the Count Donnafugata took to his bed, smudges of circles beneath his eyes, his mouth dry and crumbly at the edges, his skin tight and pale. The servants drew the thick red damask curtains across the windows and tiptoed past his door. From outside he heard the muffled, plaintive cry of loons.

## 111.

It was around this time that Jonah began to hear the fiddler play. It was a song so sweet and full of longing he thought he saw the shadows in his room rise up and dance. The notes of the fiddle rose and swooped, like birds.

The bow flew into his dreams, and the fiddler began to speak in Quaker singsong, his voice ending in a low gasp that sounded like a sob. His voice was singing in the spirit, repeating I am the Resurrection and the Life, I am the Resurrection and the Life, the Resurrection lifting upward and the Life plunging downward, the words would not let Jonah go, and all this frightening mightily Jonah, who was not easily frightened, replied:

"This music pleaseth me not."

The fiddler smiled like a sly fox and said:

"I will play what pleases me."

Jonah saw he had a wen the size of a robin's egg on the back of his neck. As the fiddler bent his head to commence playing, the wen appeared to move, rippling slowly like a snake. It slid off the fiddler's neck and slipped into Jonah's ear, saying: hear me, for I am plucked out of the air and made the ground on which you stand. And Jonah saw he was standing on the same ground where Sarah and his father had knelt and embraced to praise the Lord. A dry wind was blowing and spoke to the tindery pine needles, and from their entanglement a brush fire began to race through Jonah's heart.

112.

By this time, six months after her wedding day, Angelina had forgotten the word she once traced on the mirror's surface. She forgot the word in the same way she forgot the names of flowers. Like a river that does not know how deep its own water is or what lies beneath, Angelina did not know what names she slept with. When she awoke, she did not remember her dreams. Indeed, she did not know or ask whether she had dreamed at all. She closed her eyes and when she awoke, it was the next day, and there was absolutely no time, no gap, had passed between what had been yesterday and this day. Sleep was a cloud, and when she awoke the cloud was gone. At night Jonah made love to her, and in the morning was gone. She did not remember his touch on her skin, as tentative as fingers testing which grapes are firm and unspoiled and which are not, or his words, which were thick like honey and coated his breath. She did not remember the ways he made love to her, only that he had made love.

She did, however, remember one name and saw this name in the dark.

It was Arnaldo.

## 113.

When Jonah, that is to say the Count Donnafugata, took to his bed, he did not stay there very long as he soon grew restless and bored. It was one thing to wear yourself out looking at Angelina. It was quite another to stare at the walls and thick red curtains and hear the clock ticking away time. It was implacable. Relentless. The thought of another room came into his head. And this room would not leave him.

Jonah wanted to see again the room where Abby died. He wanted to cut her down and clutch her body like a man drowning grasps water. He wanted to see her body rise once more in his arms. And with this thought he fell asleep, and something slipped into his ear, something slipped inside him and flame-cut like Abby's voice, saying:

You didn't want to see it in any season of the year, and now the room has suddenly lodged in your heart, exactly now when you do not know what to do with Angelina.

I will not let you see it.

My death does not belong to you, nor did my life.

Jonah quit the sheets and went to Angelina.

## 114.

And one morning the Count Donnafugata woke up jubilant, the spirit singing inside him. Great news, great news flew through the wind in the pines. In the first month, it is great but small, murmured the creek as tadpoles darted back and forth. In the next few months it becomes a hummingbird. Wings beat sixty to two-hundred times a second. Chirping and buzzing, it whirs and dazzles with the display of its wings.

And finally, it is born, full of grace. Trembling on its surface, like a spider web in wet grass. Like clouds of snow in an avalanche.

Into his ear, Angelina whispered this news.

## 115.

Jonah woke up that morning, having naturally forgotten that a morning bringing great news could also spell disaster. It wasn't that he didn't remember another morning in a place whose name he had buried deep like a cache of stolen coins, a morning that started with fresh rain falling on pine and ended with the last rays of the sun slashing and twisting in the air like a knotted sheet as it cuts without mercy into the voiceless flesh of the dead. It wasn't that.

No, that morning he had rubbed with particular care the silver knob of his walking stick. He observed without comment the progress of a spider making a meticulous web in the folds of the red damask curtains. He heard the small splash of a loon dipping into the lake. And suddenly, after a long time of not remembering, remembered the empty pool of water in his dream.

Jonah wondered if he too, like his father, would spend entire days digging up the ground, wearing himself out like a fool looking for a lost cache of goods. He shivered slightly, raised the walking stick and, waving it about, he reduced the spider's web to a mesh of threads, lacking all design. Jonah saw that some of the threads were clinging to the silver knob of his walking stick.

Opening the door, he promptly forgot all of this.

In his dream the empty pool of water waited to be filled.

## 116.

Seven months later it was. This happened in April, when leatherleaf, swamp-pink, and black chokeberry bloom in the wetlands, and bird's-foot violet appears along the dry sandy roads. When the streams remember they were born in the barrens and come from nowhere else. When whip-poor-wills soar and swoop at dusk, and in the dark gypsy moths get ready to secretly devour the first leaves of spring.

All night Jonah felt suspended in a dream. The house glowed like a giant firefly, and the servants rushed from room to room in a daze. Settimo nervously burst into tears. And when at last it came, it slipped out of Angelina like a tadpole's shadow melting into dark waters. Its brown-red speckled lungs opening wide like the branching corolla clustered deep inside the gentian's purplish blue lobes. Eyes like a clouded old gravestone that does not know all writing fades. Hands clenched in trembling shock that life has offered it a fistful of freezing snow.

*Settimo*

## 117.

On the second night, Settimo received a visitor in the new house by the lake. In truth she had been waiting for him, in the dark corners of his dreams. Settimo thought he should dread her return, but instead took an odd sort of comfort as he had grown used to her company.

"You have come back."

He did not expect a reply. So he was astonished when she trembled, and tears appeared to glisten like rain on a spider's web.

"I have missed you terribly, Settimo," she said.

"Why did you leave me?"

"I do not know."

He did not know whether to believe her or not. During all the preparations for the wedding and the move to Jersey, the woman in white had abandoned him. His relief, however, was short-lived after she disappeared, and he began to feel his nerves turn jittery, almost lightheaded with the bottomless hunger that despair brings. But why should he despair? Why should he miss her? He could not explain to himself why this should be so. She was cold and, he sensed, deceitful. She made his dreams miserable. And yet she said she missed him too. He found all this confusing, but better than aimlessly roaming the streets and cemeteries of Philadelphia.

At dusk a loon cried, then dipped beneath the lake's shifting mirror of sorrow.

118.

Settimo began to take long walks in the woods. Much of the time he was alone. He did not mind being alone, which surprised him, for until then he could not have borne being apart from his wife and daughter. He did not mind, because his solitary state, he discovered, limped alongside him, and like him, snapped on crisp, dead twigs, kicked at the sugary sand, and brushed against stubborn scrub pine.

In the mountains where everything was sky he was afraid. In the barrens, he saw the vast loneliness encircling the tall grasses in the swamps, the dry sandy roads with no name, the bright yellow bog-asphodel that flowers in June. And he knew. He knew he would be forgotten.

He bent over and dug his hand into the thin, impoverished soil. Too acidic for good farming. Too leached and dry. How did anything grow here? Beneath his feet the water raced and fed the wilderness. Pools and pools of underground water that were only empty in dreams. A blue jay's explosive call cracked the sky. Settimo felt a sudden throbbing in his head. As though he were standing at the edge of understanding something very important that floated all around him. And then it slipped away, and he forgot. He forgot that he would be forgotten.

Far off, he saw two figures walking away from him. His eyes narrowed and glinted like an owl's. One of them was Angelina.

119.

In his walks Settimo sometimes thought he saw fleeting glimpses of his daughter. But on reconsidering, he realized it was more like traces of Angelina. Once it was the heavy scent of honeysuckle, and on another occasion, the whirring sound of a hummingbird's wings. In winter it was a cloud of snow. In spring, the sweet bloom of laurel in the cool air.

These traces, he knew, came from the woman flowing in white, who lent him some of her dreams, as though his own were insufficient.

What he did not know was why. Why she deposited these traces that reminded him of Angelina, as though they were carefully folded linens and garments like feathers in a wedding chest. And then departed. Only to return the following night.

He breathed deeply and found that he was happier not knowing.

For there were other things that he did know. Things that he could not tell his wife. Or Jonah.

## 120.

Settimo climbed for hours through deep clouds of thought. He was consumed by what he knew. But also bewildered, for knowing something, he discovered, did not make sorting things out any less confusing. Knowing something you wished you didn't know was like possessing a heavy stone you couldn't get rid of. No matter what you did, the stone was always there. And like all such hidden thoughts, secretly desirable. Because it was his, and no one else knew of it.

The woman in flowing white made nightly appearances in his dreams but gave no advice.

"What should I do?" he asked.

"Take this," she said and offered him a stone. It was very smooth, a nearly perfect sphere, not at all like the one he used to smash Mario's skull.

"No, I don't want it," he said, turning his head away. "Leave me alone, I don't want it." As she began to rub the stone against his wrist, he jumped up and cried: "Don't touch me!"

The stone was cool and pleasant on his skin, and this worried him even more. He felt his flesh come alive, as though some secret enchantment were glowing under its surface. The room swirled around him dizzily, and he was forced to close his eyes, but he could still see, far off, two figures walking away from him, their arms intertwined like red cedar roots. Settimo saw their kiss and felt its moist softness press against the rough, stubbled planes of his cheek, which overwhelmed him with a frenzy of longing.

He was totally unprepared for what happened next.

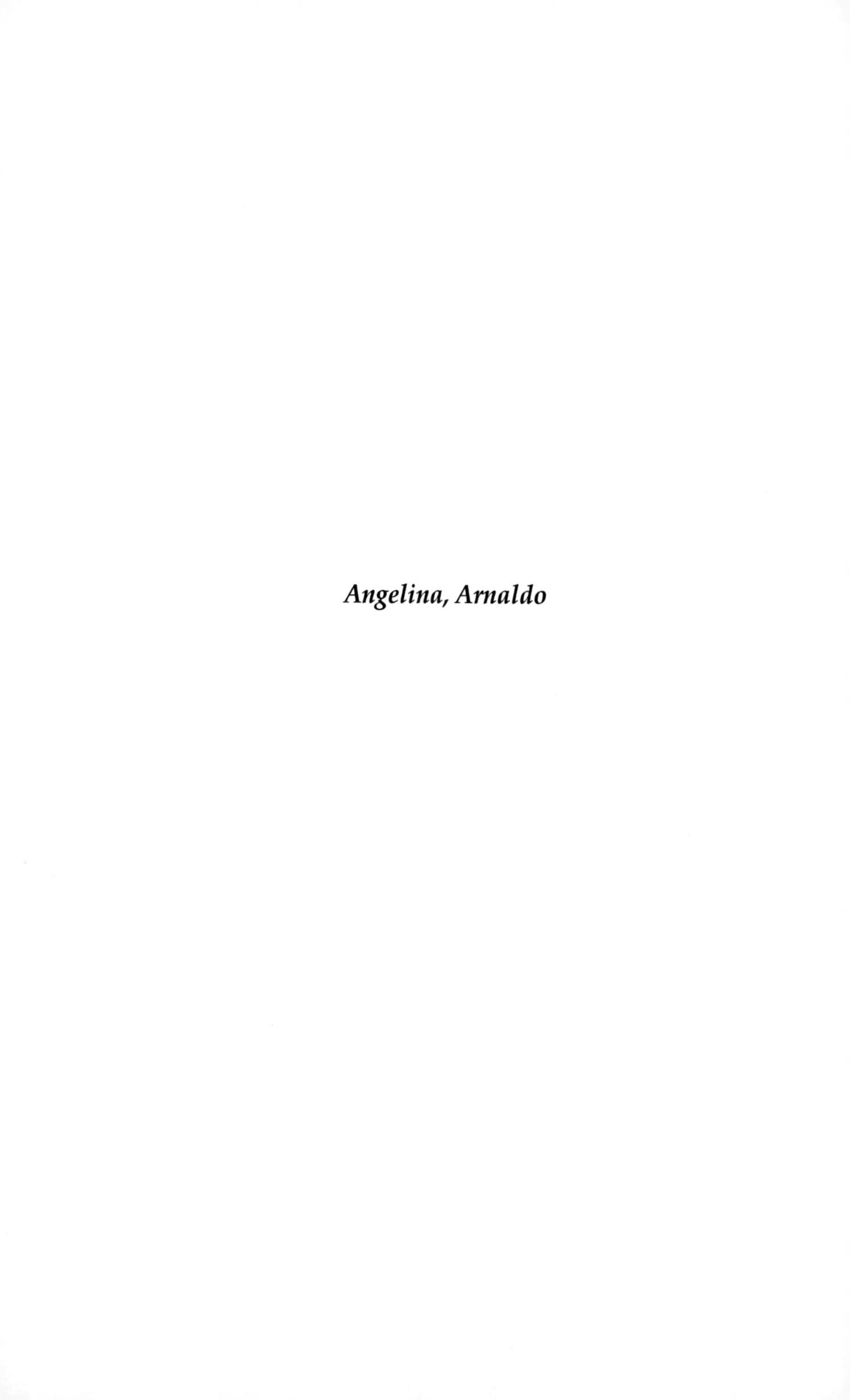

*Angelina, Arnaldo*

## 121.

Sometimes they were in the carriage house, sometimes in the barrens, sometimes speaking softly in the language that comes when a woman who cannot remember the names of flowers chooses to remember one singular name and repeats that name until she falls asleep in its arms.

The sea brought him here. The sea came in summer, like one of her father's stories, and shimmered in the distance. Angelina cupped her chin between her hands and said, yes, papa, and waited for this story to become her life.

The story walked in as an immigrant and called itself Arnaldo. Into the barrens came the spiny wild olive tree, the dark dusty figs and waving palms, the jagged earth and ash brought forth out of the long, Sicilian memory of violence. Into the barrens came his twenty-three years, which bore the scent of lemon trees floating like pale yellow specks of cloud in hazel eyes, the harsh gray rock struck repeatedly by the sun when its rays are a black, pitiless shroud, but the rock refusing to die. Into the barrens came the flowering eucalyptus tree, its thick, waxy leaves filled with the fragrance of life and glistening betrayal.

## 122.

Fed up with the stony life of Sicily, Arnaldo reached America in 1899. He was fresh, independent and tough as a knot. Therefore it was self-evident that he should end up in New Jersey, but first he went to Philadelphia where there was a thriving community of Italian immigrants. In Philadelphia he learned that one could find work in the cranberry bogs of south Jersey.

From mid-September to the end of October he picked berries by hand. At the end of four or five hours he had maybe three to four bushels, at forty cents each. At night he slept in a cedar shingled company house divided into four rooms where fifteen other Italians also stayed. Exhausted, they slept like dead men, the thick and sinewy labor of their existence plunged into some dismal, ancient stew to which they like everyone else belonged but of which they were unaware.

Working alongside them were entire families of pineys, who came with their own peck boxes and melted away like ghosts at dusk. By daybreak they were back. Bent over, they talked to each other and spent their own opinion about this and that, but to the Italians they said nothing. And the foreign men, as the people of the pines called them, because they came from inland not to mention from beyond, said nothing to them.

One night Arnaldo dreamed he was in a small boat drifting in a bank of fog. When he opened his eyes, for a moment he thought he was still there, with the patch of white that was a sail, because he could not see clearly. He heard a muffled tapping above him. Like someone was shingling on the fog.

And this was his life, until one Saturday evening there come through the fiddler.

## 123.

This was not the same fiddler come to Jonah in his dreams. This fiddler made the rounds in barns and taverns, bogs and fields. He'd set and play, then set and tell stories that were told to be true. No one knew whether it was so or not. But in the dead air of winter the fiddler's voice hung warm and welcome, and the notes he bowed were gay and sharp and the people of the pines forgot they were alone.

By mid-October the night was slowly creeping toward the deep freeze of time, when the fiddler came to the cranberry bog where Arnaldo and the other Italians were working. A bonfire roared hugely, and the pineys from nearby were there too.

The fiddler commenced to play and sing:

*If you harrow this ground with a rooster*
*And plow it with a hen,*
*You can get this money,*
*You may depend.*

And everyone nodded tapping to the tune. Some said this was "The Devil's Dream" and some said it wasn't, nobody knew that song but that anyway that was the air tune, for which the notes had never been wrote down.

"This not be the air tune," said the fiddler after playing. "I studied it but never could get it, the notes are too high, then go real low."

"I heard the notes go so high only the air can play it," someone said.

"I heard the notes go so high they get froze in the air," said another.

"Well, the way Sammy Giberson tell it, it wasn't none of that," the fiddler answered. "He heard it in a dream, woke up and played it by air." That meant it come through by ear, being the manner of saying the word in the barrens, and that was how he played it.

The fiddler drank clear, giving much pleasure to his throat and commenced to talk about this and that, which was what the people of the barrens were eager to hear, news being scarce and starless nights around them. He waited till the shank of the evening before saying what he knew. When he passed through Shamong and saw them building the big house.

"And who do you think it is for?" he asked, the corners of his mouth twitching.

There was a moment's silence while the fire made sudden snapping noises and the eyes of his listeners glimmered like water under moonlight. Then he said it. No one knew whether to believe it or not, an Italian nobleman coming to the pines. It seemed like a dream. A dream they feared would return from whence it come.

But Arnaldo took it for a sign, like the patch of white that was a sail.

That night the ghost of something small flew into the wilderness. And told him to go and find it.

124.

Arnaldo took it for a sign, and when the picking of berries was over, he went to the nearest fingerboard and stood there twenty-eight minutes. Studied the map of calluses on his hands for maybe five or six minutes more and suddenly took off. Knew where he wanted to go, but not a thing beyond that.

At Shamong he went to Buzby's General Store and inquired about work. Nothing much here besides picking, but there was a big house going up by the lake and maybe he could find something.

He was lucky. One of the men was drunk as a lark that Saturday, fell into the lake and drowned. Carted the body off in a wheelbarrow. As no one knew his last name or whence he come, the man known as Jake was buried under a slab of pine in an old graveyard, which someone sort of remembered was on a sand road off the one going to Speedwell. Speedwell itself was going nowhere, having grown down into nothing. The only thing left was the crumbling darkish remains of a furnace, a low slice of stone wall, and a pile of slag. It was like other places in the barrens, just a name beneath the pine and underbrush.

Arnaldo labored with the other men on building the house. He enjoyed this work because he could slowly see it taking shape, feeling, especially at night when his mind floated on a patch of white sail, that somehow it was also shaping the course of his life, although he did not as yet know how. In his sleep he wandered, not knowing. Not knowing that he was fate for someone else.

## 125.

By late May the sweet bay, which some call swamp magnolia, begins to blossom in the lowlands. It flourishes until early July, a fleshy stream of fragrance held in the cup of the flower's creamy-white petals and swamping the senses. It is one of the messengers of the barrens but works in mysterious ways with those who suddenly come upon it. The scent lays so thick and heavy in the air it turns the air to bones and the scent itself to tangled thighs. Water rises and floods the streets. Horses plunge recklessly into bogs and ponds. Dazed crows fly into chimneys. Keyholes stretch alarmingly and become the distended eye of the universe.

Arnaldo did not know that a person could look and look and not care and in one single moment feel his eyes were seeing like stars. Precisely at two o'clock on a Saturday afternoon in June, the Count Donnafugata, his wife and family stepped out of their carriage, like the next page in a picture book. The stable boy Arnaldo (for he had moved up in life) stood and watched as if it was one of his dreams. A small delicate foot emerged from inside the carriage and then a hand gloved in white. Clouds of black hair, a face concealed in the pallor of someone who has just woke up.

Angelina's foot stepped into a puddle of dark water that had been fresh rain falling in a curtain of chatter at sunrise. As all this happened in two seconds, she did not notice that bubbles of froth appeared to float on the water's surface. Because she looked up in that same moment. Because a thing so small as the sweet bay had suddenly bloomed.

*Jonah, Angelina*

126.

Which was why Settimo was totally unprepared for what happened next. Of course it didn't happen then, when Angelina looked up. It was later, but there is always a what happened next, even when next is just a word waiting to be written down. Or two entwined figures far off walking.

Or Jonah approaching from another sand road and suddenly seeing the same thing. Or Settimo seeing that something as small as grasping a walking stick and thinking it a fine day not to go into Chatsworth as he had planned but to wander in the woods, could also spell disaster. This was not the same day as when Jonah wondered if he too, like his father, would wear himself out looking for a lost cache of goods. It was not the same day as when he used his walking stick as a poke and wrecked the spider web. And then forgot about it. It could have been the same day, as a morning that brought great news was no guarantee of anything. It didn't make things safe. It didn't change what was next. Though the order of events could be put together in different ways, just as you might take one nameless sand road and not another of the many that crossed and crisscrossed like threads the vast loneliness of the barrens and end up in the same place. What happened next may have started with a woman who went by air and not by water. And a man who couldn't let her go. Or maybe it was earlier, when a brush fire ignited two souls but couldn't save them. Or maybe it started with murder.

It started with what happened next.

127.

Jonah saw, then hid behind a tree. Being from the barrens, he waited and kept what he knew to himself. He waited. And held the secret close to himself, as close as who he was.

Not knowing that what he knew had as much to do with who he was as anything else. He didn't exactly think about what he saw. He did everything he could not to think about it. But it was no use. At first, other things came to his mind. Suddenly he remembered his dog Red, how mysteriously the dog appeared, and how in the barrens things also disappeared in the same way. How he still loved Red, though the dog was a ghost and only raced frantically after rabbits in Jonah's mind. How things come back, even when you think they are only dreams. How you could wander for years in the wilderness like the people in his dream, who rambled up and down and wore tiny shades over their faces and didn't know why they were there and couldn't speak to you, nor you to them. How everybody he knew was buried deep inside him. How he could not bear it, not being able to speak to them. How he was wore out, just wore out, trying not to think about it. How he could be somebody else and try not to think about it. How he couldn't be himself because he couldn't think about it. How he kept thinking about it, thinking about it anyway. How the tree behind which he hid was too stunted and small to make him disappear. Or the things he had seen. I am dead, he said to himself, and as I am already dead a hundred times over, nothing I can do matters.

As the sun was setting, it pierced his eyes blinding him for an unbearable instant.

128.

This was how you made a year vanish, he kept thinking, but as everything around him seemed to be rocking like waves slapping against a boat, he couldn't remember at first which year it was. Whether it was the year after which he took to wandering and went to Philadelphia, or whether it was the year he took to marrying and returned to the barrens. By the time Jonah finally stumbled onto the sand road that led back to the great house, it was dark and the night air wore a chill. Jonah, however, did not notice, nor was he aware his body was trembling. From above an owl hooted, and a nighthawk plummeted, then soared.

At last he stood in front of his house, which glowed like a thousand fireflies. Through one of the windows he caught a glimpse of something small and white. He thought it might be Angelina. But he could not be certain, as he was some distance from the house and standing in the shadows. The longer he stood, the less clear things were. He thought of going away, of not coming back. Though he knew he could never do that. He had left once before; he couldn't do it a second time. He suddenly saw that he had staked everything on his returning to the barrens. But he had not understood until now what the stakes were.

His confusion was so great he thought he heard someone say, I am the Life. But when he turned around, there was no one. Is that you, Abby? he whispered.

I did not answer.

129.

Opening the door, Jonah promptly forgot what he thought he had heard.

You were right, husband. A wedding can come as death in disguise. You could write these words a thousand times in your copy book, and still not be prepared for my voice that is in you. My voice which is only the air of remembered flame.

That same night Angelina at last recalled the word she had traced on the surface of the mirror, saying it over and over to herself, but Jonah did not hear her. He lay rigid in bed, swallowed in darkness so thick not even his dreams could penetrate. Instead, they stood waiting like great white stags at one end of a shifting bridge they knew they could not cross.

130.

The next day, at the other end of the bridge, Angelina walked down a narrow, beaten path, which followed a winding stream of cedar water. After many twists and turns, she came to a bend where Arnaldo was waiting. The baby she was carrying had fallen asleep, so she gently laid the bundle upon a bed of moss and dead leaves. Nearby, an old rowboat rocked back and forth as the rope tugged against the current.

There was a hot, tindery wind; and as no rain had fallen for more than a month, the parched land was gasping for air. In April the stream blooms with orange-yellow spikes of golden club, which in the barrens is called neverwet, as water runs off its velvety leaves. By late July, early August, dog-day cicadas shrill and buzz, so that the pulse of the air appears to throb.

Exhausted by their own desire, Angelina and Arnaldo lay down beneath a soaring pine tree, and sleep descended like a cloud of camellias upon their dreams.

131.

But they did not dream. They woke up to their own screams, as the steady rain of blows from a dead branch fell without mercy upon them. In an instant Angelina and Arnaldo were up and running into the woods, Jonah tearing after them. His eyes focused on the point beyond, the point where he could see that Angelina, in her flight, had torn her dress, and a small white patch of it was enmeshed in a chokeberry bush.

They were running wildly, in circles, and as he knew he could catch up with them, for a moment he felt completely wore out and unable to move. He had harrowed and plowed the ground for so long, he had been so certain he would get what he had labored for with such single-mindedness, and now whatever it was, beauty, love, the mystery of grace, fled like a woman before approaching disaster. For it was nameless, like the wilderness from whence it come. And he was the disaster.

A dead branch suddenly cracked beneath his feet and brought him back to where he was, standing there, streaks of sweat running down his face, the madness in his eyes of not understanding how you could lose what you never had. He could have been standing on the same ground where Sarah and his father had knelt and embraced to praise the Lord. He could have been standing on the same ground where a man fell to his knees and begged for mercy, confessed to murder, then slept reborn for eight days straight. He could have been standing on the same ground where he labored digging a hole and thought he buried longing so deep he'd never have to see it again. But the hole was never deep enough, on that you could depend.

A dry wind was blowing and spoke to the tindery pine needles, and from their entanglement a brush fire began to race through Jonah's heart. And then, because love was a match waiting to be struck, it became faar, which was the manner of saying fire in the barrens. He saw the lit match fall, as though it had nothing to do with him, and everything he had done up to this moment receded to a faint roaring in his ears, everything but the thing for which one is never ready, the thing which came from him and which he now saw as the disaster that he was.

132.

The fire spread so quickly and so fierce, as it does in the pines, that Angelina and Arnaldo had no time to prepare, no time to outrun it.

Arnaldo clasped the form in flowing white whose lips and dark clouds of hair, pale sleeping thighs and soft eyes, he knew so little. *Io sono preso da nostalgia*, he murmured, pressing his face against her hair.

They stood leaning slightly against a pine tree. The fire come and embraced them over and over again. It leapt and burned the soles of Angelina's feet, which were bloody and scorched. Her white dress billowed and floated in the air and turned to ash. Angelina billowed and floated and turned to ash.

Fire swept over their bones.

And their bones became incandescent, and ascended in white puffs of smoke.

Something small flew out of the wilderness. Something so small that if you said, I must catch that, you wouldn't be able to, for it would come and be forgotten, would come and be forgotten before you could. Before you could remember the word Angelina had written on the mirror of her breath. Before you could open the door and still remember what your dreams said. Before the phantoms of love slipped away like glass melting in the dark.

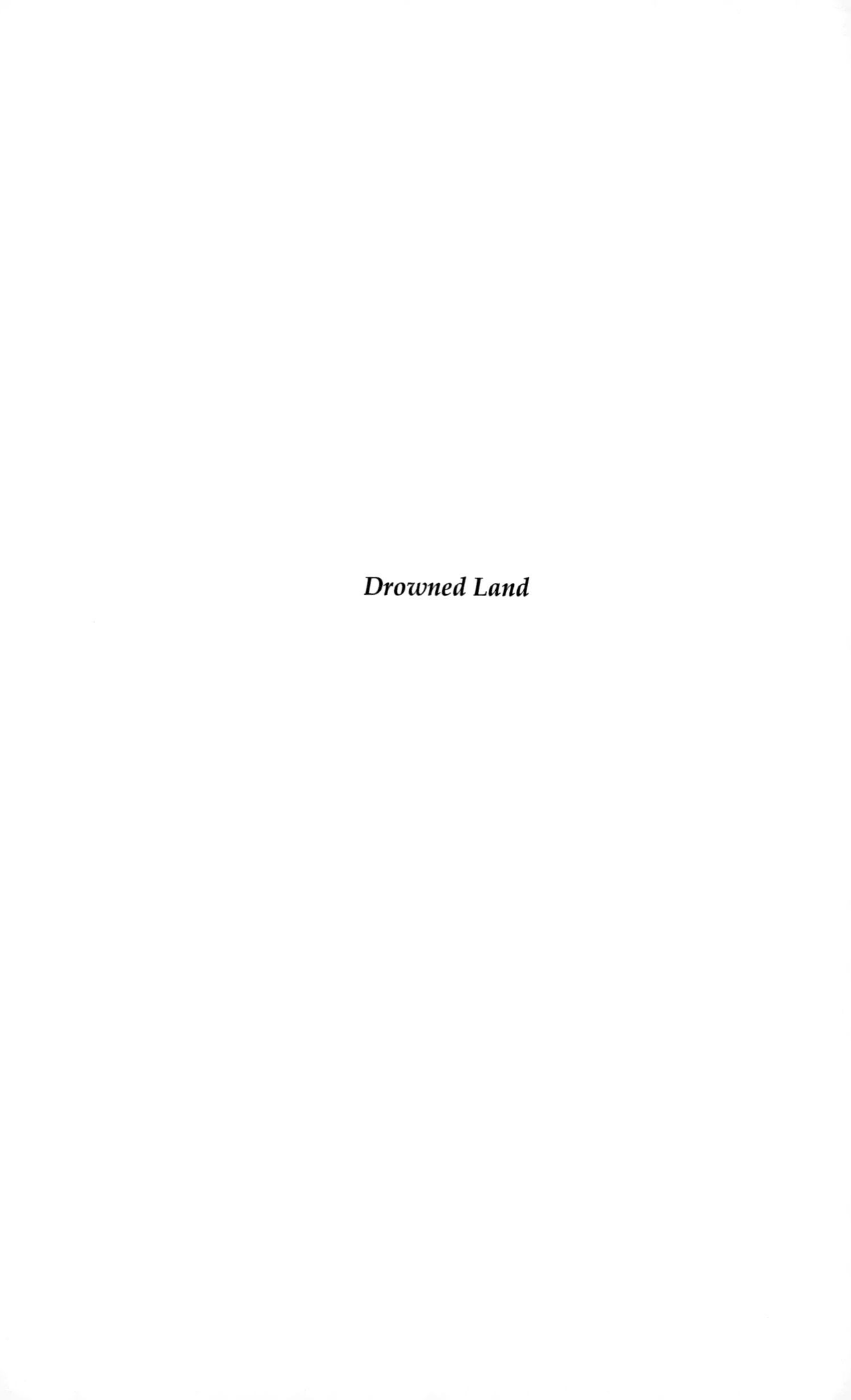

*Drowned Land*

## 133.

At that moment Jonah did remember. And raced back to the bend in the stream, the fire chasing after him. Scooped up the tiny bundle, which was wailing and red-faced. Saw he couldn't outrun the fire. Placed the bundle gently on the bottom of the rowboat, stepped in and untied the rope.

Exhausted, he lay down beside the bundle, curled up around it, closed his eyes and fell asleep. Where he saw his dream, and the dream saw him. Night came. The swirling current in which he drifted with the small white thing glinted under the rays of the fallen moon and took him to drowned land, to a marsh that lay next the stream. The wind picked up and made the reeds sing like little brushes speaking. Jonah suddenly woke up and looked down at the sleeping bundle, at the Life plunging downward, while gray ash floated like the sky in ruins around him.

He heard a voice, a voice that seemed to come from deep inside him. And it was mine, though much changed, as everything I had been was a gathering into the vast song of burned wilderness and dead towns, from which I plucked the word Angelina had written before it melted away and became the seared air of remembered flame.

Jonah stared so long at the sleeping bundle he forgot at first why he was there, or how it started with murder. And when he finally remembered, looking downward, it was his fate that he could not decide whether it should also end that way as well. At last, he lay down again and went to sleep, and in his dreams the answer came.

## 134.

In his walks Settimo sometimes thought he saw fleeting glimpses of his daughter. But on reconsidering, he realized it was more like traces of Angelina. Once it was the heavy scent of honeysuckle, and on another occasion, the whirring sound of a hummingbird's wings. In winter it was a cloud of snow. In spring, the sweet bloom of laurel in the cool air.

These traces, he knew, came from the woman flowing in white, who lent him some of her dreams, in the days when he would tremble at the thought of knowing. In the days when Settimo could not bring himself to ask her name.